D0064523

LOUISIANA'S WAY HOME

KATE DiCAMILLO

WALKER
BOOKS

First published in Great Britain 2018 by Walker Books Ltd
87 Vauxhall Walk, London SE11 5HJ

This edition published 2019

2 4 6 8 10 9 7 5 3 1

This book has been typeset in Joanna MT

Printed and bound by CPI Group (UK) Ltd, Croydon CR0 4YY

British Library Cataloguing in Publication Data:
a catalogue record for this book is available from the British Library

ISBN 978-1-4063-8558-8

www.walker.co.uk

MIX
Paper from responsible sources
FSC® C020471

For Tracey Priebe Bailey

One

I am going to write it all down, so that what happened to me will be known, so that if someone were to stand at their window at night and look up at the stars and think, *My goodness, whatever happened to Louisiana Elefante? Where did she go?* they will have an answer. They will know.

This is what happened.

I will begin at the beginning.

The beginning is that my great-grandfather was a magician, and long, long ago he set into motion a most terrible curse.

But right now you do not need to know the details of the terrible curse. You only need to know that it exists and that it is a curse that has been passed down from generation to generation.

It is, as I said, a terrible curse.

And now it has landed upon my head.

Keep that in mind.

We left in the middle of the night.

Granny woke me up. She said, "The day of reckoning has arrived. The hour is close at hand. We must leave immediately."

It was 3 a.m.

We went out to the car and the night was very dark, but the stars were shining brightly.

Oh, there were so many stars!

And I noticed that some of the stars had arranged themselves into a shape that looked very much like someone with a long nose telling a lie – the Pinocchio constellation!

I pointed out the starry Pinocchio to Granny, but she was not at all interested. "Hurry, hurry," said Granny. "There is no time for stargazing. We have a date with destiny."

So I got in the car and we drove away.

I did not think to look behind me.

How could I have known that I was leaving for good?

I thought that I was caught up in some middle-of-the-night idea of Granny's and that when the sun came up, she would think better of the whole thing.

This has happened before.

Granny has many middle-of-the-night ideas.

I fell asleep, and when I woke up, we were still driving. The sun was coming up, and I saw a sign that said GEORGIA: 20 MILES.

Georgia!

We were about to change states, and Granny was still driving as fast as she could, leaning close to the windscreen because her eyesight is not very good and she is too vain to wear glasses, and also because she is very short (shorter, almost, than I am) and she has to lean close to reach the accelerator.

In any case, the sun was bright. It was lighting up the splotches and stains on the windscreen and making them look like glow-in-the-dark stars that someone had pasted there as a surprise for me.

I love stars.

Oh, how I wish that someone had pasted glow-in-the-dark stars on our windscreen!

However, that was not the case.

I said, "Granny, when are we going to turn around and go back home?"

Granny said, "We are never going to turn around, my darling. The time for turning around has ended."

"Why?" I said.

"Because the hour of reckoning has arrived," said Granny in a serious voice, "and the curse at last must be confronted."

"But what about Archie?"

At this point in my account of what became of me, it is necessary for you to know that Archie is my cat and that Granny had taken him from me before.

Yes, taken! It is truly a tragic tale. But never mind about that.

"Provisions have been made," said Granny.

"What sort of provisions?"

"The cat is in good hands," said Granny.

Well, this was what Granny had said to me the last time she took Archie, and I did not like the sound of her words one bit.

Also, I did not believe her.

It is a dark day when you do not believe your granny.

It is a day for tears.

I started to cry.

I cried until we crossed over the Florida–Georgia state line.

But then something about the state line woke me up. State lines can do that. Maybe you understand what I am talking about and maybe you don't. All I can say is that I had a sudden feeling of irrevocableness and I thought, *I have to get out of this car. I have to go back.*

So I said, "Granny, stop the car."

And Granny said, "I will do no such thing."

Granny has never listened to other people's instructions. She has never heeded anyone's commands. She is the type of person who tells other people what to do, not vice versa.

But in the end, it didn't matter that Granny refused to stop the car, because fate intervened.

And by that I mean to say that we ran out of gas.

If you have not left your home in the middle of the night without even giving it a backward glance; if you have not left your cat and your friends and also a one-eyed dog called Buddy without getting to tell any of them goodbye; if you have not stood on the side of the road in Georgia, somewhere just past the irrevocable state line, and waited for someone to come along and give you a ride; well, then you cannot understand the desperation that was in my heart that day.

Which is exactly why I am writing all of this down.

So that you will understand the desperation – the utter devastation – in my heart.

And also, as I said at the beginning, I am writing it down for somewhat more practical matters.

And those more practical matters are so that you will know what happened to me – Louisiana Elefante.

Two

This is what happened.

We stood on the side of the road.

In Georgia.

Just past the Florida–Georgia state line. Which is not at all – in any way – a line. Yet people insist that it exists. Think about that.

Granny turned to me and said, "All will be well."

I said, "I do not believe you."

I refused to look at her.

We were both quiet for a very long time.

Three trucks drove past us. On the side of one

was a picture of a cow standing in a field of green grass. I was jealous of that cow because she was at home and I was not.

It seemed like a very sad thing to be jealous of a fake cow on the side of a truck.

I must warn you that a great deal of this story is extremely sad.

When the third truck blew past us without even slowing down, Granny said, "I am only attending to your best interests."

Well, what was in my best interests was being with Raymie Clarke and Beverly Tapinski. Raymie and Beverly were the friends of my heart, and they had been my best friends for two solid years. I could not survive without them. I couldn't. It was just not possible.

So what I said to Granny was, "I want to go home. Being with Archie is in my best interests. Raymie and Beverly and Buddy the one-eyed dog are in my best interests. You don't understand anything about my best interests."

"Now is not the time," said Granny. "This conversation is inopportune. I feel extremely unwell. But none the less, I am persevering. As should you."

Well, I did not care that Granny felt extremely unwell.

And I was tired of persevering.

I crossed my arms over my chest. I stared down at the ground. There were a lot of ants running around on the side of the highway looking very busy and pleased with themselves. Why would ants choose to live on the side of a highway where they were just going to get run over by cars and trucks on a regular basis?

Since I was not talking to Granny, there was no one in the world for me to ask this question of.

It was a very lonely feeling.

And then an old man in a pick-up truck stopped.

The old man in the pick-up truck was called George LaTrell.

He rolled down his window and raised his

cap off his head and said, "Howdy, I am George LaTrell."

I smiled at him.

It is best to smile. That is what Granny has told me my whole life. If you have to choose between smiling and not smiling, choose smiling. It fools people for a short time. It gives you an advantage.

According to Granny.

"Now, what are you two lovely ladies doing on the side of the road?" said George LaTrell.

"Good morning, George LaTrell," said Granny. "It seems we have miscalculated and run entirely out of gas." She smiled a very large smile. She used all of her teeth.

"Miscalculated," said George LaTrell. "Run entirely out of gas. My gracious."

"Could we impose upon you for a ride to the nearest gas station and back again?" said Granny.

"You *could* impose upon me," said George LaTrell.

I considered not imposing upon George LaTrell, because the truth is that in addition to being tired of persevering, I was also tired of imposing. Granny and I were always imposing on people. That is how we got by. We imposed. Also, we borrowed.

Sometimes we stole.

I considered not getting into the truck. I considered running down the highway, back to Florida. But I did not think I would be able to run fast enough.

I have never been able to run fast enough.

And by that I mean that no matter where I go, Granny seems to find me.

Is that fate? Destiny? The power of Granny?

I do not know.

I got in the truck.

The inside of George LaTrell's truck smelled like tobacco and fake leather. The seat was ripped up, and stuffing was coming out of it in places.

"We certainly do appreciate this, George LaTrell," said Granny.

Once somebody told Granny what their name was, she never lost a chance to use it. She said that people liked to hear the sound of their own names above and beyond any other sound in the world. She said it was a scientifically proven fact.

I doubted it very sincerely.

I sat in George LaTrell's truck and picked at the stuffing coming out of the seat, and then I threw the little pieces of stuffing fluff out the window.

"Stop that, Louisiana," said Granny.

But I didn't stop.

I threw pieces of truck stuffing out the window, and I thought about the people (and animals) I had left behind.

Raymie Clarke, who loved to read and who listened to all of my stories.

Beverly Tapinski, who was afraid of nothing and who was very good at picking locks.

And then there was Archie, who was King of the Cats.

And Buddy, the one-eyed dog, who was also known to us as the Dog of Our Hearts.

What if I never got the chance to use those names again?

What if I was destined to never again

stand in front of those people (and that cat and that dog) and say their names out loud to them?

It was a tragic thought.

I threw more stuffing from George LaTrell's truck window. The stuffing looked like snow flying through the air. If you squinted, it did. If you squinted really hard.

I am good at squinting.

George LaTrell took us to a gas station called Vic's Value. Granny started the work of talking Mr LaTrell into pumping some gas into a jerry can for her and also making him pay for what he pumped.

And since I had no desire to witness her efforts to get the gas that would only take me further from my home and friends, I walked away from the two of them and went inside Vic's Value, where it smelled like engine oil and dirt. There was a tall counter with a cash register on it.

Next to the cash register, there was a rack that was full of bags of salted peanuts, and even though my heart was broken and I was filled with the most terrible despair, my goodness, I was hungry.

I stared very hard at those little bags of peanuts.

The man behind the counter was sitting on a chair that had wheels, and when he saw me, he came out from behind the counter like a spider, moving his feet back and forth and back and forth. The chair made a squeaky exasperated noise as it rolled towards me.

"How do you do?" I said. I smiled, using all of my teeth. "My granny is outside getting some gas."

The man turned his head and looked at Granny and George LaTrell, and then he looked back at me.

"Yep," he said.

I considered him.

He had a lot of hair in his nose.

"How much are your peanuts?" I said.

I said this even though I did not have any money at all. Granny always said, "Ask the price exactly as if you intend to pay."

The man didn't answer me.

"Are you Vic?" I said.

"Could be."

"I am Louisiana Elefante."

"Yep," he said.

He took a yellow spotted handkerchief out of his pocket and wiped it across his forehead. His hands were almost entirely black with grease.

I said, "I have been made to leave home against my will."

"That right there is the story of the world," said Vic.

"It is?" I said.

"Yep."

"I hate it," I said. "I have friends at home."

Vic nodded. He folded his spotted handkerchief up into a neat square and put it back in his pocket.

"You can take as many of them little bags of peanuts as you want to," he said. He nodded in the direction of the peanut rack.

"Free of charge," he said. And then he rolled himself back around the counter.

Well, this was the only good thing that had happened to me since Granny woke me up at 3 a.m. and told me that the day of reckoning had arrived.

In some ways, this is a story of woe and confusion, but it is also a story of joy and kindness and free peanuts.

"Thank you," I said.

I helped myself to fourteen bags.

Vic smiled at me the whole time I was taking the peanuts from the rack.

There is goodness in many hearts.

In most hearts.

In some hearts.

I love peanuts.

Three

George LaTrell drove us back to our car and put the gas in it for us, and Granny smiled at him and called him "Mr George LaTrell, our hero," and the whole time I could not stop thinking about Vic's Value.

Because behind the counter at Vic's, there was a calendar hanging on the wall. The calendar said OCTOBER 1977 in swirly gold letters, and there was a picture of a tree covered in red leaves underneath the words. It was a very pretty tree.

But the important thing is that next to the calendar, there was a phone.

It was a green phone. It was mounted on the wall, and it was covered with greasy black finger-prints.

I should have asked Vic if I could use that phone. I felt like someone in a fairy tale who had wasted her one wish. I wished for fourteen bags of peanuts, but I should have wished to make a phone call.

And then I could have called Beverly Tapinski and asked her to come and get me.

Beverly Tapinski could figure out a way to come and get anybody.

Beverly, if you are reading this, you know it's true.

There are the rescuers in this world and there are the rescued.

I have always fallen into the second category.

We were back on the road, and even though it was October, it was hot in the car. And it was made hotter still by the fact that I absolutely refused to speak to Granny.

"You can shun me, Louisiana," she said. "You

· 25 ·

can turn your face away from me, but it does not change my abiding love for you."

I stared out the window.

"Do not worry," said Granny. "I am working towards our date with destiny, but I must tell you that I feel somewhat hobbled by my unwellness."

She cleared her throat. She waited. But I did not ask what kind of unwell Granny was.

Instead, I continued to stare out the window. I ate my peanuts one by one. And I was glad that I had taken fourteen bags of them, because there were not very many peanuts in each bag.

I did not offer to share the peanuts with Granny, because I was not, in any way, feeling generous of spirit.

"Louisiana Elefante," said Granny, "the day will come when you will regret not speaking to me."

I doubted it.

Somewhere past Wendora, Granny started to whimper.

And then the whimper became a moan.

Granny moaned so loudly that I forgot about not talking to her.

I said, "Granny, what is wrong?"

She said, "Oh, my tooth, my tooth. Oh, it is the curse of my father."

Which did not make any sense at all.

Because the curse of Granny's father is not a tooth curse. It is a curse of sundering.

But we will not speak of that now.

We slowed down. And then we went slower still. Granny moaned a great deal.

And then after a while, she pulled the car over to the side of the road and climbed into the back seat and lay down.

"Granny," I said, "what are you doing?"

"I am working to regain my strength," she said. "Do not worry, Louisiana."

I am sure that I do not have to tell you that I did worry.

Also, it didn't work. Granny did not regain her strength. She moaned louder. When I looked back at her, her cheeks were wet with sweat. Or maybe it was tears.

Although I have never in my life known Granny to cry.

"Tears are for the weak of heart, Louisiana, and it is our job to be strong in this world." That was what Granny always said.

"What do you need, Granny?" I asked.

Instead of answering me, she howled.

"Granny!" I shouted. "You have to tell me what you need!"

Granny then said one word.

And that word was *dentist*.

It was not at all what I expected her to say.

My goodness! I had been torn from my home and from my friends. There was a curse upon my head. And I was on the side of the road in Georgia with a granny who was asking for a dentist.

What could I do?

Well, I will tell you what I did.

I sat there for a minute and thought about my options, and there weren't many of them.

And that is how it came to pass that I – Louisiana Elefante – slid behind the wheel of the car and revved the engine and put the indicator on and pulled out on to the highway and went in search of a dentist.

Four

You may be surprised to learn that I had never driven a car before.

However, I had certainly spent a lot of time watching Granny drive, and I had learned some things.

I knew to lean as far forward as I could. I knew to press on the accelerator to make the car go. Also, I had a good idea of where the brake was. And steering was easy. I had no problem at all steering.

Several trucks blew their horn at me as they went barrelling down the highway, and I took this as a criticism that I was not going fast enough.

I blew my horn back at them. And then I gave it more gas. Granny was moaning in the back seat.

"Don't worry, Granny!" I shouted at her. "I am going to find you a dentist!"

She did not answer me. I believe that she was in so much pain that she had lost the ability to form words.

I had never known her to be in such a state.

I felt a wild shot of joy go through me.

I made the car go faster.

In the back seat, Granny moaned louder and then louder still.

I loved driving!

However, it came to me after some time of flying down the highway that I wasn't sure how to find a dentist.

There were advertisements for houses and hotels and pecan pies (I love pecan pies), but there were no signs for dentists.

I figured that I was going to have to turn off the highway.

According to the signage, Richford was the next town.

Richford, Georgia – it sounded like the kind of town that would have a dentist.

I took the exit.

And that is where my problems truly began.

Driving down the highway is easy. Getting off the highway is not.

At least it was not easy for me.

I knew that I needed to slow down. I knew the brake was next to the accelerator, and I moved my foot in that direction and then I pressed the brake very hard.

We came to a stop with a surprising amount of speed.

We also did a lot of spinning around.

Granny was thrown off the back seat and on to the floor.

Empty peanut bags and other items went flying through the air.

We stopped so fast that my whole life and everything that had ever happened to me flashed through my head.

I am only twelve years old, but several exciting things have occurred in those twelve years. For instance, in 1975 I was crowned Little Miss Central Florida Tire and received a cheque for one thousand nine hundred and seventy-five dollars.

Also, that same year, I almost drowned, and when I was underwater I saw the Blue Fairy from *Pinocchio*. The Blue Fairy is very beautiful. I don't know if you know this or not. She is very beautiful and very kind. And when I was underwater and almost drowning, the Blue Fairy opened her arms to me and smiled. Her blue hair was floating above her head, and there was a light all around her.

And then Raymie came and saved me from drowning and the Blue Fairy floated away. She went in the opposite direction, deeper into the pond. She looked extremely disappointed as she left.

I have never told anybody that before – about the Blue Fairy appearing to me and how sad she seemed that I was not going with her. But I am writing it down now.

There is a great deal of power in writing things down.

But continuing on with the highlights of my life: my parents were famous trapeze artists known as the Flying Elefantes. They are dead, and I do not remember them at all. I have only ever known Granny. She has been my mother and my father. She has taught me everything I know.

I have a cat called Archie.

And there is also Buddy, the one-eyed dog. He is the Dog of Our Hearts, and he lives with Beverly, but truthfully, Buddy belongs to all of us – me and Raymie and Beverly – because we rescued him together.

And of course there is the curse. The curse came about because my great-grandfather (the magician) sawed my great-grandmother in half and refused to put her back together again. Onstage. In front of an audience.

This, as you can imagine, had disastrous and far-reaching consequences.

The curse is a curse of sundering. And it is a very complicated and tragic curse.

In any case, those are the important facts of my life, and I considered them all in the long moment of the car spinning around and the empty peanut bags flying through the air.

When all the spinning and flying and considering was done, I realized that we had somehow gone entirely off the road. The car was sitting in the grass on the side of the slip road.

Granny was still on the floor in the back.

I could hear a cricket chirping. Crickets are good luck. That is what some people believe.

I sat there and listened to the cricket and thought about how driving was much more complicated than I had imagined. It turns out that many things are more complicated than I ever thought they would be.

The cricket kept singing.

There's a cricket in the story of Pinocchio.

Most people don't know this, but Pinocchio kills the cricket right in the beginning of the story. Yes, kills him — with a mallet! Whenever the cricket shows up after that, he is just a ghost.

Can you imagine being the ghost of a cricket?

That has got to be the most insubstantial thing of all.

I have to say that it doesn't seem one bit lucky to me.

Granny climbed back up on to the seat.

She sat up and looked around.

She said her new favourite word – *dentist* – and then she lay back down and moaned.

The car was still running. The engine was making some spluttery noises, but it was still going. And yes, we were on the side of the road, but I figured if I pressed the accelerator, we could get off the side of the road and continue on our journey.

And guess what?

I was right.

I pressed my foot down on the accelerator, and the car went roaring up the embankment and back on to the tarmac.

I felt proud of myself.

I continued down the road to Richford, Georgia. I drove with some caution. I kept my eyes open for a sign that said *dentist*.

Five

You have to make small plans.

That is one of the things I have discovered in this world. It is pointless to make big plans because you never know when someone is going to wake you up in the middle of the night and say, "The day of reckoning has arrived."

Days of reckoning interfere with big plans.

So I made small plans. The small plans were: keep the car on the road; find a dentist; never forgive Granny.

Although, when I think about it, never forgiving Granny would probably go in the "big plan" category.

Granny moaned. She said, "Why must you haunt me so? What do you want from me?"

She also said the word *dentist* from time to time.

I kept my mouth shut. I did not offer Granny any comfort to speak of.

And what can I say in my defence except that I was very angry and also that I was doing my best under difficult circumstances?

Finding a dentist is not as easy as you might imagine.

Nothing is.

Richford was not a big town. I went past a school and several houses and a church and also a pink cement building that had a sign outside that read: BILL'S TAXIDERMY.

How could a town have a taxidermist in a pink cement building but not have a dentist?

I saw a woman walking her dog down the road, and I felt a pang.

Who was taking care of Archie the cat?

Was he right this very minute walking down

the highway in search of me? He had done that before – found his way to me against all odds.

"Where is Archie?" I shouted at Granny.

Of course she did not answer me.

It seemed cruel to press her on the point when she was in so much pain, but as soon as she was not in pain, I intended to do exactly that: press her on the point.

In the meantime, I had to find a dentist.

I stopped the car. I did this by pressing the brake very carefully and very slowly. And when we had stopped completely, I rolled down the window and called out to the lady with the dog. I said, "Excuse me, what is the name of your dog?"

Granny moaned from the back seat.

The woman looked at me. I think she was surprised to find a child behind the wheel of a car. Well, I was surprised too.

So far, it had been a very surprising day.

"Pardon me?" said the lady.

"Does your dog have a name?"

"Ernest," she said.

"I have a cat called Archie," I told her. "And there is also a dog in my life. His name is Buddy. You will be happy to know that my friends and I worked together to rescue Buddy from a very tragic situation. Buddy is a dog who has only one eye."

"How old are you?" said the woman. Her eyes narrowed.

"That is an irrelevant question at this juncture," I said. "Isn't it?" I smiled at her using all of my teeth. "I am wondering if you can tell me where the dentist is."

"Dr Fox?"

"Certainly," I said.

"Should you be driving?" said the woman.

"I should be driving," I told her. I gave her a very serious grown-up-to-grown-up sort of look. "The situation is dire."

Granny moaned from the back seat, as if working to prove my point.

I smiled at the lady again.

Ernest the dog looked up at me and wagged his tail. Animals of every sort have always immediately trusted me. Ernest had a very handsome tail. It was burnished apricot in colour.

"I admire your tail," I said to Ernest.

He wagged it some more.

"Where is Dr Fox?" I asked the lady.

"You take a left on Glove Street," said the woman.

"And then what?" I said.

Granny groaned.

"Who is that in the back seat?" said the woman.

"That is my granny in the back seat. But continuing on with the directions – after I take a left on Glove Street, what do I do?"

"Dr Fox's office will be on your right."

"Thank you very much," I told her. "Goodbye, Ernest."

Ernest waved his impressive tail. I rolled up the window.

The whole exchange had cheered me considerably. I had located a dentist. I had met a dog called Ernest.

Also, I liked it that Dr Fox was on Glove Street. If you put the words together, they sounded like a song. I started to sing the Dr-Fox-on-Glove-Street song.

"*Where is Dr Fox?*
You take a left on Glove,
and then you continue on.
You take a left on Glove
and you sing this song."

Granny moaned from the back seat.

I got so happy singing the Dr Fox song that I almost forgot about the wrongs I had suffered at Granny's hands.

Almost.

Six

The clock in Dr Fox's office said that it was 9.47 a.m.

I was struck by how much had happened since 3 a.m.

I had been kidnapped by Granny. We had crossed over a state line. We had run out of gas. I had eaten fourteen (very small) bags of peanuts. I had seen my life flash in front of my eyes. I had met Ernest. I had found a dentist.

And I had driven the car!

"My goodness," I said to the lady behind the desk at Dr Fox's office, "would you look at the time! So much has happened."

I was going to tell her about my amazing exploits, or at least some of them, but it was very clear that the woman was not in a good mood. She was staring at me and tapping her pencil against the desk. Her lips were very thin.

"Yes?" she said.

I smiled at her.

I said, "Good morning. My granny is in desperate need of a dentist."

I expected the receptionist to say something along the lines of, "Well, you are in exactly the right place."

But she didn't say anything at all.

Instead, she bent her head and started flipping through the pages of an appointment book. I stood there and waited. The office smelled like peppermint and hand gel. There was some music playing above our heads. It was a sad and wordless kind of song.

On the desk, there was a sign with white letters that said MRS IVY.

I thought that was a very pretty name for someone with such thin lips.

"Mrs Ivy?" I said.

She looked up at me.

"It's an emergency," I said.

"Do you have an appointment with Dr Fox?"

"I do not have an appointment because it is an emergency," I said in a very patient voice. "You cannot make an appointment for an emergency, because emergencies are entirely unexpected. My granny is in a great deal of pain."

"I'm afraid that we are all booked up today," said Mrs Ivy. Her lips got even thinner.

"May I speak with Dr Fox?" I said.

"You most certainly may not," said Mrs Ivy.

There was one other person in the waiting room: an older woman who was working on a crossword puzzle and pretending not to notice that the receptionist and I were engaged in a battle of the wills.

That is what Granny called situations like this – a battle of the wills. She always told me that I could win any battle of the wills. "Your opponent will be willing to give up at some point, but you must never give up. The trick is to never give in. Be wily. And remember: no retreat. You must never retreat."

So instead of retreating, I was wily. I walked over to the waiting room and went and stood next to the crossword-puzzle lady. There was a painting above her head that showed some green trees standing together in the sunshine. In the far left-hand corner of the painting, in a dark puddle of shadow, there crouched a fox.

I stood with my hands behind my back and considered the painting. Was the fox supposed to represent Dr Fox the dentist?

"What are you doing?" said Mrs Ivy.

"I am admiring the painting," I said without turning around. "I don't need an appointment to admire the painting, do I?"

The woman with the crossword-puzzle book looked up at me and smiled.

"Hello," I said.

"Hello," said the woman.

"Are you doing difficult puzzles or easy ones?"

"They are medium," said the woman. She had a kind face. Also, doing medium crossword puzzles – not too hard and not too easy – made her seem very trustworthy to me.

"Are you willing to give your dental appointment to someone who is in desperate pain?" I asked.

"Pardon?" said the crossword woman.

"My granny needs help," I said, "and I am wondering if you would donate your appointment with Dr Fox to her."

"I'm afraid that I don't have an appointment to donate," said the woman. "It's my husband's appointment, you see. He's back there now, getting his teeth cleaned."

"You need to leave," said Mrs Ivy.

I assumed that Mrs Ivy was talking to me and not to the medium-crossword-puzzle lady, but I had no intention of leaving, and in any case, it all ceased to matter.

Because at that moment, Granny opened the door to Dr Fox's office and came staggering in with her hand to her mouth.

She was howling in a truly impressive way.

Seven

Mrs Ivy shrieked a surprised little thin-lipped shriek.

The crossword-puzzle lady stood up out of her chair. She said, "Heavens!" The crossword-puzzle book fell from her hands and landed on the floor.

"Help me," said Granny to Mrs Ivy.

"We are all booked up today," said Mrs Ivy, but she didn't sound very certain when she said it.

Clearly, the time for certainty had passed.

Granny shouted, "Argggggghhhh! Help me!" She had on her fur coat. Her hair was standing up straight on her head. Suddenly, I saw her like other people might see her, and I will not lie to you: it scared me.

How can I say this?

She did not look trustworthy.

She looked like somebody with a curse upon her head.

Which, of course, was exactly the case.

"Granny," I said.

And then a little man in a white coat came out from behind a closed door. He said, "Is there a problem here, Mrs Ivy?"

Mrs Ivy said, "There is a small scheduling inconsistency, Dr Fox. No need to concern yourself."

Granny put out her arms.

Mrs Ivy said, "Stand back!"

But it was too late. Granny went running towards Dr Fox, and when she got to him, she fell down and clutched his feet.

Well, what could Dr Fox do?

He took her into his office.

Mrs Ivy was not pleased.

She had been outwitted in the battle of the wills.

She sat down at her desk.

Her lips got so thin that they disappeared entirely.

It turned out that Granny did not have one bad tooth.

They were all bad.

That is what Dr Fox came out and told me. He stood in front of me in his white coat, adjusted his tiny glasses, and said, "I'm afraid that the infection was profound and systemic."

I looked at him and thought that he did not resemble a fox at all. He looked more like a mouse. His nose, in particular, was very tiny and mouselike. It twitched in a nervous way when he spoke.

"Profound," said Dr Fox again. "Systemic."

"Oh, my goodness," I said. I bent over. It was suddenly hard for me to breathe. I have very swampy lungs, and in times of distress, they often fail me.

Carol Anne took hold of my hand and

squeezed it. I squeezed back. Carol Anne was the medium-difficulty-crossword-puzzle lady, and we had become good friends while Dr Fox was busy pulling out each and every one of Granny's teeth.

Carol Anne was a retired librarian, and we had talked for some time about our favourite books. She was very familiar with the story of Pinocchio and even knew that the cricket was killed with a mallet at the beginning of the book.

Carol Anne was going to visit her grand-children after her husband's teeth were cleaned. She was taking her grandchildren some chocolate-chip cookies, which, when she found out how very hungry I was, she was happy to go out to her car and retrieve and share with me.

The cookies were in a red Christmas tin with a green wreath on it. There were little spots of raised-up white on the tin that were supposed to represent a joyous snowfall.

In addition to the chocolate chips, there were walnuts in the cookies, and that was a surprise. Walnuts are not my favourite nut, but they are a good nut, nevertheless.

I had eaten five walnut-and-chocolate-chip cookies. The Christmas tin was still in my lap.

I looked down at it after Dr Fox delivered his dental news to me. I ran my fingers over the raised spots of snow. I stared at the wreath. It was a very cheery-looking tin, but to tell the truth, it did not cheer me up very much to consider it. My situation was growing ever more dire.

"She will, of course, need to recuperate," said Dr Fox. "Antibiotics, painkillers and bed rest. It is quite a shock when all the teeth are removed at once."

I took a deep breath. I looked up at Dr Fox. "All of them?" I said. "There is truly not a tooth left in her head?"

Who would Granny be without her teeth? You could say what you wanted about Granny (she lied; she stole; she had a curse on her head – true, true, true), but she was, at the very least, the kind of person who smiled a lot. She used her teeth a great deal.

"Yes," said Dr Fox. "I thought it best to prepare you."

"It will be all right," said Carol Anne. She squeezed my hand again.

I wanted to believe her.

I stared at Dr Fox, the dental mouse. I looked him in the eye. I said, "Thank you very much for attending to my granny."

I noticed that there was a spot of blood on Dr Fox's white coat. It was just one little drop, and it looked like something out of a fairy tale – like a pinprick on Sleeping Beauty's finger. It made me want to cry. But then I saw Mrs Ivy sitting at her desk, looking disapproving, and I thought, *Well, I will not give her the satisfaction.*

And I did not.

And then there was the matter of the bill.

That was what Mrs Ivy said.

"There is the matter of the bill. Dr Fox's services are not free."

I said, "I did not expect them to be. You may mail the bill to us."

And on the spot, I made up a person and an address.

I said, "You may send the bill to my grandfather. He pays all our bills. His name is William Sunder. He is at 1221 Blue Fairy Lane, Lister, Florida. My granny and I are just passing through. We are on holiday."

It was deeply satisfying to lie to Mrs Ivy.

However, the satisfaction did not last long, because Granny emerged from the back room. In addition to being toothless, she looked stunned, as if somebody had hit her over the head with something very heavy.

I followed behind Granny as she staggered out the door and to the car park. I said, "Granny, Dr Fox says that you need to recuperate. I am perfectly capable of driving, as I demonstrated earlier today. You can recuperate in the back seat, and I will drive."

Granny turned and faced me and held out her hand. She said, "Give me the keys, Louisiana."

Her voice was strange – muffled and uncertain and toothless. She didn't sound like herself at all. It was alarming.

What could I do?

I handed her the keys.

We got in the car, and Granny got behind the wheel. We left Dr Fox's car park and went down the road. Granny's face was very white. She was driving slowly, staring at the road in a grim and determined fashion.

I said, "Where are we going?"

"Do not bother me with small questions, Louisiana," she said in her new disturbing voice.

Well, to me, "Where are we going?" did not seem like a small question.

It seemed like the biggest question of all.

But then I remembered that I was angry with Granny. I remembered that I was not speaking to her. And I decided that in addition to not speaking to her, I would never ask Granny a question again.

We drove until we got to a motel called the Good Night, Sleep Tight.

It was a small motel with a big sign that featured a giant neon candle and neon letters spelling out GOOD NIGHT SLEEP TIGHT. There was a painted sign in the window of the motel reception that read: *A good night's sleep is a good thing indeed.*

This was a sentiment that I agreed with, particularly since I had not had a good night's sleep the previous night – having been awoken at 3 a.m. and told that the day of reckoning had arrived.

"Are we staying here?" I said to Granny.

And then I remembered that I was not talking to her or asking her any more questions ever again.

Granny turned to me. She said, "Go inside. Use your charm and secure a room for us, Louisiana."

I stared at her. She stared at me. We stared death rays at each other. We were engaged in a vicious battle of the wills!

But after a very long time, I looked away.

Granny had won. Even without her teeth, she had won. She was still a force to be reckoned with.

I got out of the car. I slammed the door as hard as I could.

Eight

Right before I walked into the reception of the Good Night, Sleep Tight, I saw a crow sitting on the roof, looking down at me.

His feathers were very black.

"Hello," I said to the crow. He cocked his head. The sun was lighting up his wings.

Granny tooted the horn at me.

"Well," I said to the crow, "as you can see, I am not in charge here, so I guess I will have to move along."

The crow cocked his head again, and then he flapped his wings and flew away.

I still had hold of Carol Anne's Christmas cookie tin. The last thing Carol Anne had said to me was, "Sweetheart, you keep those cookies. You keep the whole tin."

As I said before, there is goodness in many hearts.

In most hearts.

Granny blew the horn again. I raised the tin up higher so that it was in front of my heart like a shield. I opened the door and went into the Good Night, Sleep Tight to use my charm and secure us a room.

What choice did I have?

The good news is that there was a vending machine in the foyer of the motel reception, and it was stocked with the most amazing array of things. There were toothbrushes with little tubes of toothpaste attached to them, and chocolate bars with caramel and nuts, and also bags of peanuts, and rain bonnets that were folded up into neat little squares, and packets of crackers with orange cheese in the middle of them.

The vending machine was such a miracle that as I stood and contemplated it, I almost wondered if I was dreaming, but then Granny blew the horn again and I knew that it was not a dream.

None of it was a dream.

I opened the second set of doors and went all the way inside the Good Night, Sleep Tight reception. There were black and red carpet tiles on the floor.

And also, there was an alligator.

He was dead, of course.

But he was dead in a ferocious pose. His mouth was open, and all his teeth were displayed.

"May I help you?" said the woman behind the counter.

Her hair was in curlers.

"Hello," I said. I smiled, using all of my teeth. "My granny is recovering from some recent tooth surgery and we need a room."

"You pay up front," said the woman. She pointed at a sign on the wall that listed the prices for rooms in red ink. It was a very emphatic sign.

"Well, my goodness," I said after I studied

the sign with pretend interest. "Would you like a chocolate-chip cookie with walnuts in it?"

"Are you selling them?"

"No," I said. "I'm sharing them."

I opened the tin and held it out to her. She took two cookies.

"This is a nice motel," I said. "I admire your vending machine and your alligator."

The woman shrugged. She said, "It's all mine and whoop-de-do and who cares? I never wanted it in the first place, especially the alligator. But that's how it goes around here. Divorce settlement. You end up with all kinds of things you don't want."

"You do?" I said.

The woman took a bite out of one of her cookies. She studied me. "Don't ask me for anything," she said.

"What would I ask you for?"

"Assistance. Mercy. I don't know. It's clear that you have a hard-luck story, and I don't want to hear it."

"Well, as I said, my granny is in the car and

she is recovering from tooth surgery. I will go and tell her that we have to pay up front. She is the one with the money."

"Tooth surgery," said the woman.

"Tooth surgery," I said. "And other tragic things have occurred, but it's probably best if I don't speak of them right now."

"Yes. Don't."

I stared at the lady, and she stared back at me.

Granny has always said that long silences make people uncomfortable and that sometimes they will say or do things that they would not normally say or do in order to fill up the silence.

However, this was not the case with the lady in curlers. I was the one who ended the silence. I said, "Do you have a phone I could use?"

"Obviously I have a phone. But you're not going to use it."

"There are probably some people who are wondering where I am," I said.

"I'm not getting involved in any of that," said the woman. She brushed cookie crumbs from her hands.

"OK," I said. "My name is Louisiana. What's yours?"

The woman narrowed her eyes. "What difference does it make what my name is? You're still not going to use the phone. And you still have to pay up front for the room."

I smiled at her.

"For heaven's sake," she said. "My name is Bernice."

I kept smiling. I said, "Bernice, do those curlers really make your hair come out curlier?"

"Why would I waste my time with them if they didn't? Go and get your granny. Nothing happens for free in this world, and I am not in the charity business, as you have surely ascertained by now."

Bernice was right.

I had ascertained exactly that.

I went out to the car to retrieve Granny.

The Good Night, Sleep Tight was a very clean motel.

I know because I looked under the bed, which is the first thing that I do whenever I go into a motel room. Before Granny and I settled into the house in Florida, we stayed in many, many motel rooms, and I kept a collection of all the things I found lurking under the beds: a spool of thread (green); a ballpoint pen imprinted with the words SCHWARTZ EXCAVATING (the ink in the pen was dried up, but I liked the word *excavating* very much); hairgrips (there is almost always at least one hairgrip under a motel bed; I do not know why this is so, but it is); paper clips; someone's letter to their uncle Al.

The letter started "Dear Uncle Al". I can't remember what it went on to say, but I was glad that somewhere in the world there was an Uncle Al. I pretended that he belonged to me and that he was the kind of uncle who pulled coins out of your ear and offered to buy you big bags of salted peanuts and candy floss on a stick when you went to a match together.

One time, in Lucas, Alabama, I looked under a motel bed and found the skeleton of a mouse. I saved that, too. I am not afraid of mice. Or their skeletons.

But when we moved into the house in Florida, and Beverly and Raymie became my friends, I threw away my collection of all the things I had found under motel beds because I thought that part of my life was over.

Well, I guess I was wrong.

In any case, the point I am making here is that there was nothing at all under the Good Night, Sleep Tight bed, not even a hairgrip.

The bathroom mirror was spotless, and the toilet had a SANITIZED FOR YOUR PROTECTION strip on it.

The water glasses were wrapped in paper.

The Good Night, Sleep Tight was very clean, and there were even two luggage racks – one for Granny's suitcase and one for mine.

Also, there was a phone in the room, but it had a tiny lock on its rotary dial so that you could not use it without a key.

Granny saw me looking at the phone and said, "Place no calls, Louisiana!"

As if I could.

And then Granny got into bed, pulled the

covers up over her head and became, to all intents and purposes, invisible.

I turned away from her and stared at the curtains, which were pushed to one side and were printed all over with little palm trees.

A crow flew by. It was the same crow that had been sitting on the roof of the motel reception. I recognized him by his shiny feathers.

"Hello," I called out to the crow.

"Close those curtains immediately," said Granny. Her head was all the way under the covers and all of her teeth were gone, but she still knew exactly what everybody was doing and could tell them how to do it differently.

It did not seem to me that her powers were diminished at all.

It was very frustrating.

I closed the palm-tree curtains. There is something sad about palm trees cavorting all over curtains when you are not in Florida but are instead in Georgia. Why weren't the curtains printed with peaches, since Georgia is the Peach State? That is what I wanted to know.

Curtains should be state-appropriate.

Lots of things, in fact, should be different from how they are.

Nine

I waited until Granny was asleep and snoring, and then I went outside.

It was late afternoon, and everything was quiet. I stood and looked at our car. Granny had the keys under her pillow, and the pillow was, of course, under her head.

But I was wily. And I believed that I was wily enough that I could steal the keys and steal the car and drive back to Florida.

However, I didn't know what direction Florida was.

Well, it was south, of course.

But how was I supposed to know which way was south? How could you possibly tell which way south was when there were so many directions in the world? Northeast. Southwest. People can point, and study maps, and say the words "south" and "east", and look very knowledgeable when they say them, but directions have always confused me.

And there was also the fact that I didn't have any money for gas. Or food.

And then, too, how could I leave Granny alone in a motel room with no teeth and no car?

It seemed cruel.

I was thinking about all of this when someone whistled, and the crow – that same crow – went flying past me in a burst of shiny feathers. He was so close that I could feel the air he pushed aside.

I looked up, and lo and behold, what did I see?

A boy. Standing on the roof of the Good Night, Sleep Tight.

And the crow was sitting right on the boy's shoulder.

"Hey," said the boy. He was barefoot. He had

on blue shorts and a white T-shirt, and his hair
was cut so close to his head that it was bristly and
shone in the light.

"Hello," I said back.

"You know that vending machine in reception?"

"Yes," I said.

"I seen you staring at it earlier."

"So?"

"So, I can get you any old thing you want out
of that machine. Anything at all. All you got to do
is name it."

Well, my heart soared up high in my chest at
those words. I saw the vending machine as if it
were right in front of me. It glowed with all of
its special objects – ballpoint pens, cheese-filled
crackers, chocolate bars, rain bonnets – each one
of them giving off its own special light.

"My goodness," I said to him.

"Anything you want." He smiled. He looked
like a pirate, standing up there with the crow on
his shoulder.

And then Bernice came out of the motel

reception with a broom in her hand and the curlers still in her hair.

"How many times do I have to tell you?" she shouted, waving the broom around. "Get off my roof! Get off it!"

Bernice jabbed the broom at the roof. She jumped up and down.

"Get out of here," said Bernice. "I mean it."

"I'll see you later," said the boy, looking right at me. "Go on, Clarence."

The bird (Clarence!) took off flying; the boy went running across the roof and grabbed hold of the branch of a big oak tree that was next to the Good Night, Sleep Tight, and then he was gone too.

"Don't believe a word he says," said Bernice, turning to me.

But it was too late.

I believed him entirely. I believed everything about him.

I couldn't wait to make my selections from the vending machine.

And then two things struck me at once. The

first was that I knew the bird's name but I did not know the boy's.

The second thing that occurred to me was that I felt hopeful.

Yes. For the first time since we had crossed over the Florida–Georgia state line, I – Louisiana Elefante – was filled with hope.

Ten

My hopefulness did not last long.

It turned out that Granny had paid for only one night at the Good Night, Sleep Tight, and at eleven o'clock the next morning, Bernice was knocking at our door saying, "You will pay now, or you will get out. Thank you very much."

Her hair was still in curlers.

"I am recovering from a traumatic event," said Granny in her new toothless voice. She stood at the door in her nightgown. Her legs were skinny and white. She looked like a troubled ghost.

Bernice said, "I have absolutely no interest in

hard-luck stories. I am interested in you paying for another night, or I am interested in you packing up and leaving. One thing or the other."

Granny said, "Very well. I do not have cash. But I do have Louisiana."

"What?" said Bernice.

"Louisiana," said Granny, "come here."

I went and stood in front of Granny. She put her hands on my shoulders. I could feel her fingers trembling. I had never known Granny to tremble. And her hands were hot. It felt like she was on fire.

"She sings," said Granny to Bernice.

"So what?" said Bernice.

"She sings like an angel," said Granny.

I stood there with Granny's trembling, feverish hands on my shoulders, and I felt a wave of darkness and despair roll over me.

What would become of us?

What would become of me?

I thought about the boy on the roof and the crow called Clarence and the vending machine stocked full of wondrous things.

I thought about Beverly and Raymie.

I thought about Archie and Buddy.

I missed them. I missed them all.

I wanted to go home.

But who cared what I wanted? Certainly not Granny.

Which is how I ended up at the Good Shepherd Lutheran Church wearing my best dress in preparation for singing to someone called Miss Lulu, who was the church organist and who had made up her mind in advance not to be impressed with me.

And that was fine, because I was certainly not impressed with her.

When Bernice and I arrived, Miss Lulu was playing the organ. She was pounding her way through a song by Bach, and I felt sorry for Bach because Miss Lulu's heart was clearly not involved with the music at all. It was very painful to listen to her play.

Your heart has to be involved with the music, or else there is no point. That is what Granny has always told me, and I believe it to be true.

Also, Miss Lulu was eating a chocolate caramel while she played the organ. I could smell it. It is not at all professional to eat a caramel and play the organ at the same time.

Miss Lulu made us wait until she had played the Bach all the way to the end. And then she turned and said, "Good afternoon, Bernice."

"Hello, Miss Lulu," said Bernice. "Here we are, although I am not sure exactly why."

Bernice had a somewhat confused look on her face.

It was because she was dealing with Granny. I had seen the look on the faces of many people. Bernice was wondering just exactly how she had been talked into what she had been talked into.

Granny had a strange power over people, even without her teeth.

"Tell me the story about this child again," said Miss Lulu, working the caramel around in her mouth.

Miss Lulu had curls in her hair. The curls bounced when she talked.

Curls – or the hope of them – seemed to be

very popular in Richford, Georgia.

"Well," said Bernice. She sighed. "She and her grandmother are staying at the motel, and they cannot pay for another night."

"Isn't that just terrible?" said Miss Lulu. "Some people." She tossed her head, and the curls bounced up and down and the smell of chocolate and caramel wafted through the air.

I do not believe that people should eat chocolate without sharing it.

There was a stained-glass window above Miss Lulu's head, and if I squinted at it, I could turn all the colours in the window into a kaleidoscope and also make Miss Lulu's face and curls go fuzzy, so that is what I did and it was very comforting.

In the meantime, Bernice went on talking. "The grandmother says that the girl can sing. She says that I can make money having the girl sing at funerals and weddings. And since you are the one who plays the organ at the weddings and funerals, I thought I would give you a call and, well, here we are."

Miss Lulu looked me up and down.

I looked her up and down back.

She had on snagged stockings. Her nails were bitten down. So what if she had bouncy curls?

"Well," said Miss Lulu, "it doesn't seem probable, does it? She looks like something blown in by a storm."

Bernice sighed. "I know it. And Lord help me, you should see the grandmother. I feel like I am being hoodwinked. And I am not a fan of being hoodwinked. One time was enough."

"Yes. Well, Bill was a piece of work. And love makes us do foolish things," said Miss Lulu. "But you did get the motel."

Bernice made a huffing noise.

Miss Lulu said, "The truth is that there are often requests for someone to sing at a funeral, and since Idabelle Bleeker passed, there hasn't been anyone with the voice to do it."

"Is there a phone that I could borrow, Miss Lulu?" I said, hoping to achieve success by a surprise attack. I had seen the minister's office on the way into the sanctuary. The door was closed, but there was a sign that said:

MINISTER'S OFFICE
REVEREND FRANK OBERTASK
ASSISTANCE, ADVICE, HEALING WORDS

I was not particularly interested in receiving Assistance, Advice, or Healing Words.

But every church office has a phone. I could go into the office of Reverend Obertask and pick up the phone and call Beverly or Raymie and have them come and get me!

"What?" said Miss Lulu.

"I need to call somebody," I said.

"Ignore her," said Bernice. "She's odd."

To me, she said, "We did not come here for you to place phone calls. We came here to see if you can sing."

Miss Lulu crashed out a few chords on the organ.

And then she said, "We will perform 'Just a Closer Walk with Thee.'"

Well, that is a song I know.

Miss Lulu started to play, and I opened my mouth and sang. I sang as if my life depended on it. Which I guess you could say it did. Or at least my room at the Good Night, Sleep Tight depended on it.

I sang as if the Blue Fairy from *Pinocchio* was smiling at me. I sang as if Beverly and Raymie and Archie and Buddy could hear me and would use the song to find their way to me. I sang as if I knew the name of the boy on the roof. I sang as if he knew my name, too.

The Georgia sun shone in through the stained-glass window. At some point, Miss Lulu stopped playing the organ and just sat with her hands on the keys and looked at me.

There was a big splotch of orange on her face from the stained glass and a splotch of green lighting up one of her many curls. All of this was good, because it made her look somewhat friendlier.

I kept singing.

Bernice was crying. Tears were rolling down her face.

The world smelled of unshared chocolate caramels and dust and beeswax. Everything was broken; I knew that. But I felt like I could fix it if

I just kept singing. And so I kept singing.

It is good to have a talent in this world.

When I had finished, there was a long silence.

Bernice snuffled. She said, "Bless her heart. I guess you can never say what riches people contain."

And then Miss Lulu asked me if I liked sponge cake.

I told her that I most certainly did.

My goodness, who doesn't like sponge cake?

The three of us went down to the social hall, and Miss Lulu gave me a piece of cake on a china plate that had little pink flowers all around its rim. It was a very pretty plate.

I sat on a metal folding chair that felt cold against my legs, and I ate the whole piece of cake without bothering to talk in between bites.

Miss Lulu and Bernice watched me.

"Who taught you to sing?" said Miss Lulu when I'd finished eating.

"My granny," I said. I picked at the sponge cake crumbs on my fork.

Miss Lulu nodded. Her curls bounced up and down.

"Do you use curlers, or is your hair naturally curly?" I asked.

Miss Lulu stared at me with her mouth hanging open. It was as if I had asked her to solve the most difficult maths problem in the world. I was starting to think that she was not a very bright woman.

Miss Lulu turned and looked at Bernice and said, "There is a funeral on Friday. Hazel Elkhorn. I am playing the organ. I am sure that the Elkhorn family would like someone to sing."

Bernice nodded slowly. Her face was puffy from crying. "I guess we will start there and see what happens. How much should we charge?"

And since I was finished with my sponge cake, and since it was almost as if I were invisible to them as they did their planning and cogitating about how to make money from me, I stood up and said, "Excuse me, I will be right back."

I went up the stairs and out of the social hall and knocked on the door of Reverend Frank

Obertask's office, and when Reverend Obertask did not answer, I opened the door and went inside, and there it was: a phone. Sitting on the desk. Just as I thought it would be.

My heart beat very fast.

My salvation and rescue were at hand!

Eleven

In addition to my heart beating fast, my lungs felt swampy.

I bent over and put my hands on my knees and breathed deep. I looked around the office. It was filled with books. They were piled up on the desk and on the floor. The walls were lined with shelves and the shelves were jammed tight with books.

My goodness, it was a lot of books.

Whoever Reverend Frank Obertask was, he certainly believed in the power of the written word. And that was fine by me, because I believe in the power of the written word too. For instance, I believe in these words I am writing, because they are the truth of what happened to me.

I considered the power of the written word while I breathed deep and got my lungs calmed down, and then I stood up straight and stepped over to the desk and picked up the phone, and there was a dial tone.

Everything was going exactly right.

But there was one small obstacle.

The one small obstacle was that I did not know Raymie's phone number.

Or Beverly's.

I did not know their numbers because I had never called them.

Granny did not believe in having a phone in the house.

She said it was just one more way for the authorities to keep tabs on us. "What do we need a phone for, my darling? The general populace does not need to know our whereabouts, and those who love us can always find us."

That is what Granny said.

But it's not true, is it?

Those who love us can't always find us, can they? Or else I would not be writing these words.

There are always and for ever obstacles placed in our path.

But I had a plan to overcome at least one obstacle! I was going to request operator assistance.

I picked up the phone and dialled, and a woman came on the line immediately and said, "Directory enquiries. What city, please?"

"Lister, Florida!" I shouted the words. I felt like I was on an important game show and that I had to answer very quickly and exactly right.

"Name?"

"Raymie Clarke, and there is an *e* on the end of *Clarke*!"

There was a long moment of silence.

"There are five listings for Clarke. None of them is Raymie. Would you like to try another name?"

"Yes!" I shouted.

"What other name, please?"

"Beverly Tapinski!"

"Please spell the last name," said the operator.

I spelled it, and then there was a long, sad silence.

The operator cleared her throat. She said, "I am sorry, dear, but there are no Tapinskis in Lister, Florida."

"Yes, there are," I said.

"Well, perhaps there are," said the operator. "But there are no listings for Tapinskis."

"But they exist. Beverly Tapinski and Raymie Clarke both exist. What do I do now?"

"Regarding what?" said the operator.

"Regarding me not knowing who to call," I said.

"This is directory enquiries," said the operator.

"I know that," I said. I stamped my foot. "But I don't know what to do. You should assist me and tell me what to do."

"Honey," said the operator, "it will all be fine."

And then there was a click and she was gone.

I hung up the phone. I bent over and put my hands on my knees and worked to get air into my lungs.

I thought, It will not all be fine.

I thought, I am alone in the world, and I will have to find some way to rescue myself.

Twelve

When I got back to the Good Night, Sleep Tight, the palm-tree curtains were closed and the room was dark and Granny was still in bed.

"Granny?" I said.

"Mmmpph," said Granny without moving or removing the covers from her head.

"Granny!" I said in a louder voice.

"I am very tired, Louisiana," said Granny. "I am unwell and baffled and compromised. I would like to sleep."

And I said, "Well, sleep away. I will be singing at a funeral, and that means we can keep staying in this motel and you can sleep and sleep and sleep."

Granny moved the tiniest bit. She said, "Do not bother resenting me, Louisiana. I have always put you first in this world. I am trying to protect you. I am working very, very hard to protect you. It is just that I am so tired..." She said all this without taking her head out from under the covers. Her voice was muffled. It was as if she were talking to me from a long, long way away. It was as if she had moved to a different country, a country without teeth.

"I want to go home," I said.

Granny threw the covers off her head. It was the first time I had seen her face-to-face in what seemed like a long time. She looked different – smaller and less certain. Her mouth was caved in. Her cheeks were flushed. She glared at me.

Truthfully, she was somewhat frightening to behold.

"Louisiana Elefante," she said, "we are not going home."

I glared at her.

She glared at me.

I looked away first.

I said, "I'm hungry."

"You are always hungry," said Granny in a relieved voice. She put the covers back over her head. "Yours is a perpetual and unceasing hunger. Go and find some food. I am working to regain my strength. Do not forget the curse, Louisiana!"

How could I forget the curse? My great-grandfather sawed my great-grandmother in half on a stage in Elf Ear, Nebraska, and then refused to put her back together again. That is not the kind of thing you forget.

It may not be the kind of thing you want to face, but it is also not the kind of thing you forget.

I left the room and went and stood in the foyer of the reception of the Good Night, Sleep Tight. I considered the vending machine.

Of course, I was hoping that the boy on the roof would show up and offer to get me whatever I wanted, but I was starting to think that maybe I had imagined the boy. Just as maybe I had imagined the Blue Fairy holding out her arms to me the time I almost drowned.

Had I imagined the Blue Fairy?

I could not say for certain.

Had I imagined the boy?

I did not think I had.

I knew for a fact that I did not imagine the crow called Clarence, because he had been sitting on top of the Good Night, Sleep Tight sign when I stepped out of my room.

"Hello, Clarence!" I had shouted at him.

He had nodded and looked down at me in a very kingly way.

He was probably pleased that I had remembered his name.

In any case, the crow was real and the vending machine was real, and I stared at it and thought about what I would get if I could get anything I wanted.

I could see Bernice inside the reception, sitting at her desk. Her hair was in curlers. What a surprise. I waved at her. She pretended not to see me.

If the boy showed up and offered to get me

whatever I wanted, I decided that I would select a packet of peanut-butter crackers and a packet of crackers with cheese, and one of the ballpoint pens (so that I could continue to write everything down), and also an Oh Henry! chocolate bar because I like the name of them, how upbeat and hopeful they sound. And also, because they have caramel in them. And peanuts. Which is a very good combination.

I was thinking all of that when the door to the foyer opened and there he was.

The boy.

"Hey," he said.

Oh, my goodness, I was glad to see him.

I was glad even beyond the contents of the vending machine. And by that I mean that I liked his face and I was glad he existed – even if he couldn't get me the crackers and the pen and the chocolate bar.

"I thought maybe I had made you up," I said to him.

"Naw," he said. He stood there, holding the door open, smiling. He nodded in the direction of

Bernice. "She don't like me," he said. "Any minute now and she'll be out here with her broom, trying to chase me off. Come on."

The minute we stepped outside, Clarence came swooping down from the sign and landed on the boy's shoulder.

I had never seen such black and shiny feathers. The crow stared at me and I stared back at him, and looking into his eyes was like looking in a dark mirror.

I felt that if I looked carefully enough, if I held myself still enough, I would be able to see the whole wide world reflected in that shiny blackness. Almost.

"Would he sit on my shoulder?" I said.

"I reckon if he gets to where he trusts you, he would."

Clarence flapped his wings and took off, past the sign, towards the trees.

"What's your name?" said the boy.

"Louisiana," I said. "What's yours?"

"Burke. Burke Allen. But I ain't the first Burke Allen. My daddy is Burke Allen and my grandpap is Burke Allen and his daddy before him was Burke Allen, and his daddy, too. There've been a lot of Burke Allens."

"Well, as far as I know, I am the only Louisiana Elefante."

"That's lucky, then. You ain't got to be nobody but yourself."

I said, "I have a curse on my head."

I don't know why I said it. I shouldn't have said it. Granny has always insisted that we not talk about the curse to other people.

"To speak of the curse only intensifies the curse." That is what Granny said.

Granny said a lot.

For as long as I could remember, Granny had been talking to me, telling me things, and telling me not to tell things.

I had never told Raymie about the curse. Or Beverly. But here I was telling this boy I did not know at all.

Maybe, in addition to being tired of imposing

and persevering, I was also tired of keeping my mouth shut.

"A curse," said Burke. "Dang."

"Yes," I said. "It's a curse of sundering."

"Of what?"

"Sundering."

"I don't know what that is."

"It means to tear apart," I said.

"All right," he said. "If you say so." He pointed at the Good Night, Sleep Tight sign. "See that sign?" he said. "I can climb all the way up to the top of that sign. I can show you how, too."

"I'm afraid of heights," I said.

"Shoot," he said. "There ain't nothing to be afraid of."

"I don't want to fall."

"You can't fall because there's little bitty hand-holds the whole way up. You just have to hold on and climb. I can show you how to climb up on the roof, too. Ain't nothing to it."

"No," I said.

He waited, and I waited. His almost-not-there hair glinted in the sunlight.

"Why is your hair so short?"

He shrugged. "My mama cuts all our hair. My daddy and my grandpap and me. She cuts it all the same."

"So your mother cuts the hair of Burke Allen and Burke Allen and Burke Allen?"

He smiled. "Yeah," he said. "All of us."

"My parents are dead. They were trapeze artists."

"In a circus?"

"No," I said. "They had their own show. They were famous. They were called the Flying Elefantes."

"I want to be in a circus," he said. "First chance I get, I'm going to join a circus. Circus trains come through here sometimes. You ever seen a circus train?"

I shook my head.

"They're all on it. All of 'em. The whole circus. Elephants and clowns and giraffes and trapeze people. Next time that train comes through here, I am going to hop on it – can't nobody stop me." He sighed. He looked up at the motel sign.

Here he was, right in front of me, and already he was telling me how he was going to leave. It was the curse of sundering. I would never be free.

Suddenly, I felt terrified.

And also annoyed with Burke Allen.

"I thought you said you could get me anything I wanted out of the vending machine."

"I can."

"Good," I told him. "I want the cheese crackers and the peanut-butter crackers and an Oh Henry! bar. And also a pen. To write with."

He grinned at me. "I'll be right back," he said.

A few minutes later, he came running out of the reception holding two packets of crackers and an Oh Henry! bar.

"I didn't get the pen," he said, "on account of I didn't have time. Bernice is right behind me, and she ain't happy."

Well, Bernice was never happy, was she?

"Come on," he said. "We got to run."

I ran with him. We ran into the woods. At some point, Clarence showed up and he flew over our heads and cawed and cawed. He was laughing as if somebody had just told him a joke.

Crows have a good sense of humour.

I ran with Burke and Clarence, and I forgot about Granny being toothless and diminished. I forgot about Miss Lulu and how badly she played the organ and how she refused to share her chocolate caramels. I forgot that there were no phone listings for Raymie Clarke or Beverly Tapinski. I forgot that I had to sing at Hazel Elkhorn's funeral.

I forgot that I was far from home.

I ran.

Thirteen

We sat out in the woods under a tree, and Clarence perched on one of the branches above us and his dark feathers shone over us.

"It was in Elf Ear, Nebraska, in 1910," I said.

"What was?" said Burke.

"The curse," I said. "That is when it all began."

"I ain't never heard of Elf Ear, Nebraska. It sounds like some made-up place."

"I am telling you a story that I have never told to anybody else," I said. "If you intend to listen to it, you can't doubt everything I say. Otherwise, there is no point in telling you."

I had eaten the entire packet of peanut-butter crackers and most of the crackers with cheese. I intended to eat the Oh Henry! bar for dessert.

"Dang, you was hungry," said Burke.

"I am perpetually hungry. That is what Granny says."

"I can make you a tinned-meat sandwich if you want," said Burke. "My house ain't far from here."

"Tinned meat is what they eat in the county home, and the county home is the place of no return."

Burke shrugged. "I don't know about the county home."

"Granny has been warning me about the dangers of the county home my whole entire life."

"OK," said Burke. "All I'm saying is that I can make you a meat sandwich if you want one. If you're still hungry."

"Well," I said.

I was. Still hungry.

"Come on," said Burke. "You can tell me about the elf ears later."

"Elf Ear. It's a place. Elf Ear, Nebraska."

"Yeah," he said. "Come on. Let's go to my house and make a sandwich."

I ate the Oh Henry! bar while I walked behind Burke through the woods. The bar was chocolatey and caramelly, and it was maybe the sweetest and best thing I had ever eaten in my entire life.

I started to feel somewhat hopeful about the universe and my place in it. Even if I was headed off to eat tinned meat – favourite of the county home, food of despair.

I love tinned meat!

Burke made me three sandwiches. They had tinned meat and orange cheese and mayonnaise in them and they were on white bread, and he stacked the sandwiches up one on top of the other and put them on a blue plate, and we sat in the dining room at a glass-topped table, and I ate the sandwiches one by one without stopping.

Granny had always spoken poorly of tinned

meat, but these sandwiches tasted so good that it was just one more reason for me to doubt Granny and the truth of her utterances.

And by that I mean this: if you are the kind of person who lies about something as small as tinned meat, what would stop you from lying about bigger, more important things?

Burke stared at me while I ate. "Dang, you can eat a lot."

"Granny says I need to keep my strength up," I said.

"That's your granny? That old lady who don't never come out of the room at the Good Night?"

"Yes. She recently had all her teeth pulled. She is working to regain her strength."

Burke nodded.

From the glass-topped table in the dining room, I could see over a field and into the woods. It was late afternoon, and the light was fading. Sometimes, when the light starts to fade, I get a terrible feeling of loneliness, like maybe I am the only person in the world.

One time I confessed this to Granny, and

she told me that I shouldn't take everything so personally. She said, "Louisiana Elefante, the light has been fading since the dawn of time, and it will continue fading long after we are gone. It has nothing to do with you."

Still, it makes me sad when the light goes.

Burke sat across the table from me. There was the sound of a clock ticking, and from outside, I could hear a crow cawing.

"Is that Clarence?" I said to Burke.

"Yeah," he said. "He gets mad when I'm inside the house for too long. He misses me, I reckon."

"I am very far from home," I said.

"Well, all right," said Burke. "Where's home?"

"I am now going to tell you the story of the curse," I said.

"OK," said Burke.

"I need to tell you this story."

"OK," said Burke. "I'm listening."

"It was in Elf Ear, Nebraska, and the year was 1910, and my granny was eight years old, and her father was the most elegant and deceitful magician who ever lived."

"Your granddaddy was a magician?" said Burke.

"My great-grandfather," I said. "And my great-grandmother – my granny's mother – was the magician's assistant. They travelled all over the country. They performed magic together."

"It was like being in a circus," said Burke.

"It was like being in a magic act," I said. "But what matters is that I am telling you about the curse. And the curse began on a stage in Elf Ear, Nebraska. My great-grandfather pulled my great-grandmother out of a hat – a small hat. He made her appear. And then he made her disappear back into the hat. Just like a rabbit!"

Burke was staring at me, listening. He had very blue eyes.

"What happened next?" he said.

"What happened next was that my great-grandfather uttered the fateful words 'I will now saw my lovely wife in half and put her back together again, for I am Hiram Elefante the Great.'"

"That was his name? Hiram Elefante the Great? What kind of name is that?"

"It was his name," I said. "The important thing is that the magician's assistant climbed into the box and Hiram Elefante nailed the box shut. And then he took a saw, and he sawed the box in half. With my great-grandmother in it! She was cut in two! Sundered! Do you understand?"

Burke nodded. "Yeah," he said. "It was a magic trick. He sawed her in half, and then he put her back together again."

"Well, that is what the audience thought would happen. That is what everyone anticipated. But it was not what happened."

I stared at Burke, and he stared at me.

"Well?" he said. "What happened?"

"My great-grandfather sawed my great-grandmother in half, and then he walked away. He left my great-grandmother on the stage. Sawed in two. He walked out of the theatre in Elf Ear, and he kept walking. No one ever saw him again."

"But what about your great-granny?"

"Someone else put her back together, a man

from the audience who knew some magic, and then the two of them ran away together and my granny was left entirely alone."

"Dang," said Burke. "Is this a true story?"

"Of course it's true!"

"What happened to your granny?"

"She got sent to the county home, to an orphanage. And that is the story of the curse of sundering and how it has been passed down through the generations. And now that curse is on my head."

"Well," said Burke, "what you got to do is undo the curse, right? That's what I would do."

"Undo it?" I said. "How would I do that?"

"I don't know. There's got to be a way. Maybe what you do is you go and find you another magician to work some magic — different magic. Magic that puts things back together."

Outside somewhere, Clarence called out. Burke and I sat there and stared at each other, and even though I was filled with crackers and tinned meat and an Oh Henry! bar, I felt very empty and sad.

Could the curse really be undone?

I doubted it.

I don't think Burke Allen fully comprehended the depth and breadth of the curse upon my head.

"I suppose I should go back and check on Granny," I said. "Maybe she is hungry. Maybe you could make her a tinned-meat sandwich."

"All right," said Burke.

I didn't know if Granny would eat a tinned-meat sandwich. In fact, a tinned-meat sandwich might enrage her. Maybe I was hoping to enrage her. I don't know.

But in any case, Burke went into the kitchen and came back out a minute later with two tinned-meat sandwiches wrapped up in a paper towel.

I was starting to see what kind of a person he was.

He was the kind of person who, if you asked him for one of something, gave you two instead.

We went back outside and stood in front of Burke's house, which was painted as pink as candy floss on the outside. It was all by itself in the woods, with no other houses nearby. Burke whistled and Clarence came flying out of the woods and landed on Burke's shoulder. And I thought to myself that my life would never be truly complete until I could whistle and have a crow come flying out of the trees directly to me.

"There's going to be a carnival at the church on Saturday," said Burke. "A carnival ain't a circus, but it's still something. And it is mostly fun. There's rides and games."

"Oh," I said.

"You and me could go."

"I need to know something," I said. "This is important. What direction is south from here?"

Burke pointed without even having to stop and consider. It was very impressive. "That way," he said. "Why?"

I turned and looked south. Clarence raised his wings and lowered them, but he stayed on Burke's shoulder.

"Why?" said Burke again.

"Because south is where Florida is," I said.

"So?" said Burke.

"Florida is where I am from. That's where my friends are. That's where Archie the cat is. That's where Buddy the dog is. And that is where I need to get back to."

"How do you aim to get there?"

"I don't know," I said. "I will figure out a way. I am wily and resourceful. According to Granny."

We started to walk back to the Good Night, Sleep Tight. Clarence flew ahead of us, stopping to wait on tree branches, looking down at us and laughing and laughing.

Maybe crows are right about the world.

Maybe everything is funny.

Fourteen

Speaking of funny – when I walked into Room 102 of the Good Night, Sleep Tight and said, "Granny, I have brought you two tinned-meat sandwiches!" Granny did not say anything at all.

I expected her to curse the very existence of tinned meat. Or to tell me that she was not hungry.

But Granny said nothing.

"Granny?" I said.

I went over to the bed. I pulled back the covers.

Granny was not there!

I have never been so surprised in my life.

"Granny?" I said in a very loud voice.

I looked in the bathroom. I looked under the bed.

And then I ran out of Room 102 and looked for the car.

And guess what? It was gone!

I went back into the room and saw that Granny's chequered suitcase was not on her luggage rack. I felt dizzy. The whole room was spinning. I couldn't breathe.

Where would Granny go without me? I was the reason for her existence. She had told me so many times. She said that what kept her alive was looking out for me and teaching me to make the most of my gifts.

I bent over and put my hands on my knees. I took deep breaths. I looked around the spinning room.

And that is when I saw it.

An envelope.

With my name on it.

. . .

Inside the envelope, there were several folded-up pieces of paper.

I unfolded them very, very slowly.

Dear Louisiana.

Those were the words written at the top of the first page.

It was a letter.

Granny had written me a letter.

She had never before written me a letter.

And why in the world would she write me a letter? From the very first minute of my life that I could recall, Granny was with me and I was with her.

Why would you write someone a letter when you were always and for ever by their side?

You wouldn't.

Unless, of course, you intended not to be by their side any more.

I opened the palm-tree curtains and sat down on the bed and stared out the window. I heard a rustling. Was it wings? Was Clarence the crow somewhere near by? Had he come to save me?

And then, my goodness, I realized that the rustling was the letter. My hand was trembling, and the pages of the letter were brushing up against each other.

It was at this point that I understood that a tragedy was in the process of occurring.

The sky outside the window of the Good Night, Sleep Tight was blue-black, and the curtains had palm trees instead of peaches, and Granny was gone, and I could feel the world whizzing past me.

I once had a teacher called Mrs McGregor who said that the world was turning very slowly on its axis.

"It is moving infinitesimally," said Mrs McGregor.

Infinitesimally.

She said the word very slowly. She stretched it out – in-fin-it-esss-i-mally – so that you could hear the *infinite* in the word when she said it.

Mrs McGregor always had dried spit in the corner of her mouth, but she was a very patient woman and she was a truthful person. I liked Mrs McGregor. I could not imagine her telling a lie.

But here is the thing: it did not feel to me like

the earth was moving infinitesimally. It felt like it was hurtling and jerking its way through a lonely darkness.

To my way of thinking, you never knew when the earth was going to lurch and go somewhere entirely unexpected. There was nothing infinitesimal about it.

I guess that is what the curse of sundering will do to you if it has been placed upon your head – it will change how the earth itself moves.

Oh, Raymie and Beverly.

Oh, Archie and Buddy.

Oh, Granny.

I looked down at the letter in my trembling hands.

I started to read.

Fifteen

Dear Louisiana, I read. *You must be brave.*

Well, that first sentence made me mad.

I was tired of being brave. Just like I was tired of imposing and persevering.

But I went on reading.

I am going to tell you some things you must know, that perhaps you should have known all along.

I could feel my heart sink all the way down to my toes.

I knew it. I knew that this was a letter of goodbye; I could tell. It was almost more than I could bear.

But I had to bear it, didn't I? What choice did I have?

I read on.

I know that you know the story of the curse, but what I have never told you is that I saw my father that night – the night that he sawed my mother in half and walked away without putting her back together again.

I was standing at the window of the hotel room. I was waiting for the two of them to return from the theatre. I was up late, later than I should have been. I looked out the window of the hotel room, and I saw my father walking down the street towards the hotel. He was alone. His magician's cloak was floating out behind him. And I knew, suddenly, that he was going to tell me something important, but I did not know what it was. I could not imagine, you see. I could not imagine.

My father stopped and looked up at the window of the hotel. I waved at him. He looked at me, and then he turned and walked away without saying anything to me at all.

And that moment, when my father left without

telling me anything, is the moment when the curse truly began.

That was the true moment of sundering.

I closed my eyes. I could see small Granny, young Granny, standing at the window of the hotel room watching her father turn and walk away from her. It made my heart hurt. Poor Granny.

At least she had all her teeth then.

I read on.

In these last few days, my father has appeared to me again and again. In Florida, I woke from a dream of him calling my name (speaking to me at last!), and I knew then that we must go to Elf Ear immediately. That is why we left in such haste, Louisiana. I felt as if I was being summoned.

And now every time I close my eyes, I see him, my father. He appears out of the fog of my mind and he calls my name and his tone is ominous. It has become clear to me what I must do. I must go and confront the curse. I must do it alone.

Was it a good idea for a toothless, feverish Granny to go and confront the curse by herself?

Without me? Well, I did not think so. But then, Granny wasn't soliciting my opinion, was she?

I don't know what I will find in Elf Ear, Louisiana. I don't know what darkness awaits me, but I know that I must keep you safe from it.

I wish that I could say goodbye to you in person, but I fear that you would insist on coming with me; worse, I fear that I would not have the courage to go.

And I must go.

Oh, I do not want to leave you as my father left me. I want you to know that you are loved. I want to tell you the truth of who you are.

Brace yourself, Louisiana.

I looked up. I stared at the palm-tree curtains and the dark world outside. I braced myself.

Your parents were never known to me.

"What?" I said out loud. I looked around Room 102. "What are you talking about, Granny? Of course my parents were known to you. My parents were the Flying Elefantes. They were famous far and wide. They were beautiful and talented. You have told me so many times."

You and I are not related at all, Louisiana.
We were tossed together by the winds of fate.
Your parents were not the Flying Elefantes. They
were not trapeze artists. I do not know who your
parents were. That is a mystery I will not be able
to unravel for you.

Something large and dark had entered
Room 102 of the Good Night, Sleep Tight, and the
large, dark thing was sitting right on top of my
chest. I could not breathe.

If my parents were not the Flying Elefantes,
then who was I?

"Read on," whispered the dark thing on my
chest. "Read on."

After the curse befell me, I was sent to the
county home. And after the county home, after
I survived that miserable, miserable place, I
entered the world as an adult; I moved through
it as a solitary being, and I did not mind at all.
I was glad to be alone. Yes, glad. For if you are
alone, then you do not need to worry about the
curse of sundering.

I had a certain musical gift; when I was very

*young, my mother had taught me to play the
piano. And so that is what I did. I played the piano
at churches. I gave recitals and lessons. And I
worked at other jobs, small jobs – clerking, typing,
cashiering.*

I got by.

*Listen, Louisiana, listen. Now we come to you.
When I lived in New Orleans, I worked for
a time at the Louisiana Dollar Store.*

I sat up straight.

The dark thing on my chest sat up straight too,
but it did not go away from me.

*One evening, I walked out into the alley and
I heard the whimper of a small animal.*

I knew what was coming.

"Read," the dark thing said. "Read."

I read.

It was you, Louisiana.

*You were impossibly small. You were wrapped
in a flowered blanket. Someone had put you on top
of a pile of cardboard boxes and left you there.*

*Understand, I had never wanted a child. I had
no need to rescue anyone.*

But I picked you up. And you smiled at me.
You smiled, Louisiana.

I knew what it meant to be abandoned, left
behind.

I knew, too, what would happen if I notified
the authorities. I knew that you would go to the
orphanage, to a county home.

I could not let that happen.

So this is the truth. These are the facts:
I picked you up. You smiled at me. I named you
for where you were found, and caring for you has
been the greatest joy of my life.

I was named after a dollar store?

I was not an Elefante?

Someone had left me in an alley?

I couldn't breathe.

I would give anything to stay here with you,
but the curse will not be denied. See how it is even
now doing its dark work and pulling us apart?
Please understand: I am old and I am very unwell
and I fear there is little time left to me.

My father will not stop calling my name!
I must go and face the curse! I will try to

return, but in case something prevents me, in case my time is too short, I want to tell you this: do not come after me. The curse is too dangerous!

I wish that I had time to see you to safety, but you are wily, resilient. You are not alone in the world. You will find a way. And please remember this: someone put you down in that alley, but I picked you up. And perhaps what matters when all is said and done is not who puts us down but who picks us up.

I have loved you with the whole of myself, Louisiana. You will always and for ever be loved by me. I have gone to Elf Ear to set us both free.

Do not forget that you can sing.

I love you.

Sixteen

"Get off me," I said to the dark thing on my chest. "Please get off me."

But it did not move.

I stood up. I kept hold of the letter. I picked up the tinned-meat sandwiches, and I staggered out of Room 102.

I went into the reception of the Good Night, Sleep Tight, because I did not know where else to go. Bernice was behind the counter. A tragedy was occurring, the darkness had descended, and Granny was gone, but Bernice's hair was still in curlers.

Here is something I have learned: you should

never expect help from someone who perpetually has their hair in curlers.

But what was I to do? Where could I turn?

I didn't even know who I was.

"Good evening," I said to Bernice.

"What now?" said Bernice.

I guess that it was just impossible for her to be a friendly person, no matter how hard she tried.

Not that she was trying.

"I am wondering if you have seen my granny recently and if she gave you any information," I said.

"Seen your granny?" said Bernice. "What information? Don't tell me your granny is missing."

"She is not missing," I said.

"Then why are you looking for her?" said Bernice. She narrowed her eyes.

I narrowed my eyes back at her, but the dark thing was still on my chest and it was very hard for me to breathe.

I turned away from Bernice. I bent over and put my hands on my knees. I closed my eyes and concentrated on breathing.

Who am I? Who am I?

That was the question my heart kept beating out.

When I opened my eyes, I saw the alligator staring at me. He was an incredibly ferocious-looking alligator, but he also seemed perplexed – as if he were thinking, *How in the world did a dangerous man-eating alligator like me end up dead in the reception of the Good Night, Sleep Tight motel?*

There is something very sad about contemplating a perplexed stuffed alligator when it is dark outside and you do not know who you are or who your parents were or anything about yourself at all.

"What are you doing?" said Bernice.

Well, yes. That was the question, wasn't it?

"I am communing with the alligator," I said.

"Oh," said Bernice. "You're communing with the alligator. Of course you are. I suppose next you'll be speaking with the vending machine. And that reminds me. Let me tell you something about Burke Allen and that vending machine. He makes little coin-shaped pieces of metal down at that machine shop of his father's, and then he puts the metal into the vending machine and takes what he wants without paying for a thing. That is theft. That is a crime."

Burke!

Burke called Allen, who gave me two sandwiches when I had only asked for one.

Burke Allen, who had a crow called Clarence.

I could feel the dark thing on top of me lifting up, peeling away. Burke Allen would help me. Burke Allen would know what to do.

I stood up straight. I turned around and faced Bernice.

"Thank you very much," I said.

Even though she had not helped me with anything at all.

"Be polite up to the last minute. Be polite until they absolutely force you not to be." That was what the woman called Granny always advised.

I left the Good Night, Sleep Tight reception and I did not look back.

Seventeen

How hard could it be to find a pink house in the woods?

Well, it turned out to be harder than I expected.

To begin with, it was dark and I could not see where I was going. And there were trees everywhere and tall grass and mean bushes. Also, it was unnecessarily windy.

Something was flying over my head, and I do not think it was a bird.

Under the best of circumstances, I have never been able to tell one direction from another. And these were not the best of circumstances.

I kept hoping that Clarence would appear and lead me to the pink house and to Burke Allen. In the story of Pinocchio, Pinocchio is lost and walking through the woods and a blind cat and a lame fox come along and tell him a lot of lies.

I made up my mind that I was not going to listen to anyone who told me lies.

Of course, thinking about lies made me think about Granny.

That is, I thought about the woman who I had once believed to be my granny, even though she was absolutely no relation of mine.

I can tell you one thing: whoever she was, she was certainly a big old liar!

I was never ever going to speak to her again, and I hoped that she remained toothless until the end of time.

Oh, I was mad.

And also, I was lost.

And then I fell into a hole.

*   *   *

It was not a deep hole. And that was fortunate. But it was deep enough to make me lose my balance and fall to the ground and drop the letter and the tinned-meat sandwiches.

I stood up. My ankle hurt. So I went back down on my hands and knees, and I crawled around in the dark woods looking for the letter and the sandwiches.

And because it was dark, it was hard to find anything.

And my goodness, I was lonely. I almost wished that a blind cat and a lame fox would show up, even if they were just going to tell me lies. It would be nice to have some company.

I crawled around some more and found both sandwiches. That was a good thing.

But I could not find the letter. The wind had taken it away. It was gone, gone, gone.

Just like Granny.

I started to cry.

* * *

I cried and cried. But since who knew what was

going to happen next (I certainly had no idea) and since it seemed like a good idea to keep my strength up in such a dark and windy world, I ate one tinned-meat sandwich and then I ate the other one.

I cried the whole time I ate them.

Both sandwiches were very good.

Imagine Granny lying to me about tinned meat!

She should have put something in her letter apologizing for all the lies she had told me – including the lies about tinned meat.

And then I remembered that Granny was not my granny and that I had lost the letter informing me of that fact.

I stood up, but it still hurt to stand on my ankle, so I went back down on my hands and knees and I crawled over the ground looking for the stupid letter. I started to cry harder and louder. It was very hard to breathe, and everything smelled like tinned meat and a little bit like orange cheese.

The world was so dark! I don't know that I had ever before encountered such darkness.

So you can imagine how surprised I was when a bright light shone out of the darkness and a voice said, "What in the world…?"

I stared into the light. I said, "I am looking for a letter and a pink house and a boy called Burke Allen."

And then I fainted.

The next thing I remember is being carried.

I smelled something sweet.

I said, "What is that smell?"

A man's voice answered me. He said, "That's cake, darling."

I liked that answer very much. I think that "cake" is a very good word in general and that people should use it as an answer to questions more often.

"Darling" is a nice word too.

The cake smell got stronger and sweeter, and then I saw the pink house. And I was so happy that I must have passed out again.

Just from sheer joy.

Eighteen

When I opened my eyes, I was on a red-flowered couch and three faces were looking down at me. One of the faces belonged to Burke Allen.

"She ain't no bigger than a minute," said a man with very short grey hair.

"Her name is Louisiana Elefante," said Burke. "And her mama and daddy was trapeze artists."

"I thought she was some kind of wounded animal," said the third person. He looked just like Burke, except older. His hair was blond too, and cut just the same as Burke's and the old man's.

"I thought maybe she was a bobcat," said the

blond man, who was surely Burke's father. "She was wailing like a bobcat."

"There ain't no more bobcats in them woods," said the grey-haired man.

"I know that, Daddy," said Burke's father. "I'm saying that's what she *sounded* like."

"Well, she ain't no bigger than a minute."

"You already said that, Grandpap," said Burke.

"I'm saying it again, ain't I?"

"You are all Burke Allens," I said, because it was just now making sense to me. One Burke Allen was the father and the other Burke Allen was the grandfather, and the final Burke Allen was my Burke Allen.

Burke looked down at me and smiled. "Hey, Louisiana," he said.

I stuck my hand up and waved at him.

"Hey," said Burke again. "How do you feel?"

"I feel strange," I said.

"Maybe it's that old curse," said Burke.

"What curse?" said the grandfather.

"There's a curse upon her head," said Burke.

"Now, son," said Burke's father, "don't go making things up."

"I ain't making it up," said Burke. "She told it all to me."

"Where is Clarence?" I said.

No one answered me.

The cake smell was very strong. The couch was flowery. Did I say that already? My ankle hurt, but not much. I felt like I was floating on a flowery, cake-scented cloud.

Maybe I was in heaven.

"Granny" didn't believe in heaven. But that didn't mean I had to not believe, did it?

Maybe I came from a long line of believers. Who could say?

In any case, the cake smelled very, very good.

"What kind of cake is that I smell?" I said to Burke.

And then there was a woman coming towards us. She had big blonde hair. She was smiling at me. She didn't look a thing like the Blue Fairy, but she smiled the same way the Blue Fairy smiled. She was wiping her hands on a striped teatowel.

She said, "Honey, that is my famous chocolate-chocolate cake."

Burke said, "Mama is making seventeen cakes."

"Seventeen?" I said.

"Seventeen," she said.

Seventeen cakes!

The room spun around.

"Burke," I said, "I don't know who I am."

"You're Louisiana," he said.

"Did she hit her head?" said his mother.

"There's a letter," I said. I tried to sit up, but I felt dizzy, and I immediately lay back down. "The letter explains everything. Actually, it doesn't explain anything at all. And besides, the letter is gone, blown by the wind into the lands of no return."

"How's that?" said the grandfather. "The lands of what?"

"We'll find it," said Burke.

"I don't want to see that letter ever again," I said. I started to cry.

"She's crying," said Burke.

"I see that, son," said Burke's father.

"Hey now," said the grandfather. He took hold of my hand, and his hand was so rough and calloused and oversized that it was like holding on to a horse hoof. I cried harder.

I had never held hands with a horse before.

"Thought she was a bobcat," said Burke's father.

"No bigger than a minute," said the grandfather. He squeezed my hand with his horse hoof. It hurt, but it was comforting, too.

"Burke," I said, "Granny is gone."

"Gone?" said Burke.

"Gone," I said.

The world smelled so sweet.

I thought I would just close my eyes.

Nineteen

When I woke up, it was morning and the sun was shining and I was in a bed and covered by a big fluffy quilt.

There was a beside table next to the bed. On top of the beside table, there was a lamp with flowers painted all over the shade. And beside the lamp, there was a red plate with a sandwich on it. And the sandwich had some ham in the middle!

This was exciting because I was very hungry.

I sat up.

There was a glass of orange juice on the beside table too. And there was a note.

The note said:

> *Honey, here is some breakfast. I thought*
> *you should go on sleeping. Burke is at school,*
> *and Burke's daddy and granddaddy are at*
> *Burke Allen Machinery. I am at Maribelle's*
> *salon. I will call and check on you at*
> *lunchtime. Don't worry about a thing.*
>
> *From your friend, Betty Allen.*

It was the nicest letter I had ever received.

It was certainly nicer than what Granny had written to me in her letter.

"Granny" – that person I did not know at all, that person I was not even related to.

I heard a tapping against the window. I looked up, and guess who it was?

Clarence the crow! He was sitting on Burke's shoulder and leaning forward and tapping the window with his beak. Oh, I wished I had a crow to sit on my shoulder and tap on windows! I just knew it would change my whole life for the better.

Burke was smiling and waving at me. I waved back at him, but my heart was heavy. What was I going to do? I couldn't imagine.

I truly couldn't.

Burke and Clarence disappeared, and there was nothing outside the window except trees and woods and a cloudy sky. Granny's letter was blowing around out there somewhere in that world.

Well, I hoped those pages blew as far away from me as possible. I hoped those words of hers were blown by the winds of fate all the way to China.

That's what I hoped.

And speaking of being blown by the winds of fate, where was I going to go? What would become of me? I could not seem to escape the curse of sundering.

Burke walked into the room, still smiling, and I looked into his blue eyes, and that is when I recalled his words from the day before about finding a magician who could undo the curse.

And then I remembered the sign on Reverend Obertask's door:

MINISTER'S OFFICE

REVEREND FRANK OBERTASK

ASSISTANCE, ADVICE, HEALING WORDS

Wasn't a minister like a magician?

Weren't healing words like a spell?

Maybe Reverend Obertask knew some healing words that could undo the curse!

I didn't need that Granny person to undo the curse. And besides, I was finished entirely with counting on her. I would just get it done myself. I would get everything done myself.

"Do you know where the Happy Shepherd Church is?" I said to Burke.

"The Good Shepherd?"

"Yes. That one."

"Sure, I know where it is. Why?"

"We need to go there."

"What for?" said Burke.

"Because I am going to take action," I said.

"Don't you want to find the letter you was talking about last night?" said Burke.

"I do not," I said. "I don't care if I never see that letter again."

"Also, last night you said your granny was gone."

"That doesn't matter either," I said, "because I have a plan."

"All right," said Burke.

I picked up the ham sandwich and took a bite, and my goodness, it was delicious.

"Aren't you supposed to be at school?" I said to Burke.

Burke shrugged. "I skipped. I skip all the time. It don't matter. What do I need school for? You don't need school to join the circus."

Outside the window, I could see Clarence. He was looking at us, cocking his head first one way and then the other. I thought, *Wouldn't it be nice to be a bird and to have feathers and not to have a care in the world?*

But Clarence probably had cares.

Because that is what it means to be alive on this infinitesimally spinning planet. It means you have cares.

Doesn't it?

"Why are you limping like that?" said Burke.

We were walking into town.

"Because in a tragic moment of darkness and despair, I fell into a hole," I said.

"Oh," said Burke.

We walked over train tracks. Clarence kept flying ahead of us and then flying back, looking down and laughing.

"This is where I seen the circus," said Burke. He stopped walking. "Right here. I was sitting on my grandpap's shoulders. I was – I don't know – maybe six years old. We watched the whole circus go by on the train. The giraffes had their heads sticking up out of the carriage. There was lions, too. Two of them. You could smell them. They was pacing back and forth in a cage. And there was this clown. His face was all painted up, and he waved at me. And that is when I decided that I was going to join up with the circus."

"If you join the circus, you have to travel all the time," I said. "You have to leave everyone behind. The circus is just one long goodbye."

"How do you know?" said Burke. "And besides, I want to go out there and travel all over and see everything there is to see. I can always come back home if I want to."

"If I had a mother who was baking seventeen

cakes, I would want to stay right where I was," I said.

"Yeah, well. Them cakes ain't for me. They're for the carnival, for the World-Famous Betty Allen Cake Raffle."

"I have never heard of the World-Famous Betty Allen Cake Raffle."

"Shoot. You haven't? I tell you what — people come from all over Georgia just to try and win one of Mama's cakes."

For the rest of the way into town, Burke Allen told me all about the World-Famous Betty Allen Cake Raffle and how Miss Lulu played piano music before each raffle number was called and how one year a woman was so excited about winning that she fainted dead away when Betty Allen called her number.

It sounded fascinating. Except for the part where Miss Lulu played piano. That was not fascinating at all.

"Is there a limit to how many cakes you can win?" I asked.

"It's a game of chance," said Burke. "There

don't got to be a limit, because it ain't nothing but chance."

I thought that I would have to tell Granny about the World-Famous Betty Allen Cake Raffle, because it was exactly the kind of activity she would be interested in. Imagine winning a whole cake! And then I remembered that Granny was gone, that she had left me. And that she was not my granny at all.

Was I ever going to get used to the fact that I had been lied to and abandoned?

Well, I just could not say.

All I knew was that my heart was broken into several hundred pieces, and I was walking along beside Burke Allen and dreaming of cakes as if the world were a normal place.

Clarence was flying ahead of us, his wings shining in the light.

The world spins on, just as Mrs McGregor said it does. It spins infinitesimally and it never, ever stops.

Somewhere up above us, Clarence laughed. I couldn't see him.

But I could hear him laughing.

. . .

We walked past Bill's Taxidermy. And we walked past Dr Fox's office. I thought about Mrs Ivy sitting at her desk typing out a bill and sending it to a person and an address that did not exist, and that made me happy.

"Down that road is Burke Allen Machinery," said Burke. "That's where Grandpap and Daddy are right now. Working on machinery. That's what they do all ding-danging day long. They like working on machinery.

"And right there is the church," he said, pointing. "You see it?"

"Yes," I said. "I see it."

"Me and Clarence will wait for you in the woods. I got to keep a low profile. I can't let nobody see me skipping school."

And so I walked into the Happy Shepherd by myself.

I walked up the stairs, and there was Reverend Obertask's office, just where I remembered it being, just where I had left it.

I knocked on the door.

No one answered. I turned the knob and opened the door and, my goodness, there he was: Reverend Obertask.

He was asleep. His feet were on the desk, and he was tipped back in his chair with his big arms hanging down on either side of him. His glasses were crooked on his face, and his mouth was open, and his face was covered in whiskers.

Reverend Obertask looked very much like a walrus and not one bit like a magician.

The Georgia sun was shining into the office. It was lighting up all of Reverend Obertask – his nose and his sideburns and his moustache.

I stared at him, and then I stared directly into the light. It occurred to me that the Georgia sun was different from the Florida sun. I knew that it was the same sun – of course I did. There is only one sun, no matter where you go on this infinitesimally spinning earth. That is a fact.

But there are facts and there are facts. And one fact is that it is the same sun, and another fact is that if you are far from home, and you don't know who you are, it is a very different sun.

I was standing there thinking all of that when I noticed that Reverend Obertask had a pipe in his right hand.

And the pipe was dangling so low that it was almost touching the carpet.

Reverend Obertask, the walrus-magician, was going to inadvertently set fire to the Sweet Shepherd Church!

Twenty

I went very quickly and very stealthily into the office.

"Reverend Obertask?" I said.

He made a little snorting noise.

And then he dropped his pipe.

Dropped it!

I immediately bent down and picked up the pipe, thereby averting a gigantic and tragic church fire. In the meantime, Reverend Obertask slept blissfully on.

I was standing there, holding the pipe and staring at Reverend Obertask, when who to my wondering eyes should appear?

Miss Lulu.

Of course.

She was standing right at the entrance to the office. She had her hands on her hips. "What in the world is going on?" she said in a very loud voice.

Well, that has never been an easy question for me to answer in any situation because so much goes on in this world.

I stared at Miss Lulu and her curls. I smelled caramel. Did she have an unlimited supply of chocolate caramels?

"I am unsure exactly what you are referring to," I said. "And I do not care for your implications."

"I just bet you don't!" shouted Miss Lulu.

And then Reverend Obertask woke up.

"Harrrrruuummmpph," he said. "Must have drifted off."

"Well," said Miss Lulu, "explain yourself."

"Just a midmorning nap, Miss Lulu," said Reverend Obertask. He took his feet off the desk and put them on the floor. "I don't know that it can really be explained beyond that – just a middle-aged man trying his best to make his way through this vale of tears."

"I was talking to the child," said Miss Lulu. "The one who is holding your pipe."

"My pipe?" said Reverend Obertask. He blinked.

I stood up straighter.

I said, "Hello, Reverend Obertask. Here it is. Your pipe." I held up the pipe. "I came in here to ask for assistance and advice, and also to make some enquiries about your healing and magic words, but you dropped your pipe, and I picked it up so that there would not be some tragic fire. I did not want the Tiny Shepherd Church to go up in flames."

"My healing and magic words?" said Reverend Obertask. "What tiny shepherd?" He blinked again. He was a man with a very round and very surprised face. Also, he had a great deal of facial hair.

"I hate to say this—" said Miss Lulu.

"I would advise against saying it, then," said Reverend Obertask.

But there was no stopping Miss Lulu.

"I think she was intending to steal your pipe," she said.

"I was not intending to steal your pipe!" I said. I stamped my foot. "I do not need a pipe!"

Miss Lulu said, "Be that as it may. The child and her grandmother are staying at the Good Night, Sleep Tight. They are just passing through – if you understand my meaning. The child sings. And she is engaged to sing at the Elkhorn funeral tomorrow. But I'm worried that something, uh, *untoward* is occurring. Or will occur."

"Untoward?" said Reverend Obertask.

"Exactly," said Miss Lulu.

"Thank you very much, Miss Lulu," said Reverend Obertask. He sat up straighter. His chair creaked. "You may leave us."

"But, Reverend," said Miss Lulu. "The child has your pipe."

"Yes, she does," said Reverend Obertask.

Miss Lulu sighed a very large sigh. The smell of caramel drifted across the room.

"I will take it from here, Miss Lulu," said Reverend Obertask. "Thank you for your generous insights and kind intervention. Goodbye."

"Goodbye, Miss Lulu," I said. It was a sentence that I liked saying very much, so I said it again. "Goodbye, Miss Lulu."

"Yes, goodbye," said Reverend Obertask. "And please close the door behind you."

Miss Lulu stood there with her mouth hanging open and her curls holding themselves very still. And then she pulled the door closed in a huffy and important way, and I was alone with Reverend Obertask, the walrus who could maybe perform magic.

I was certainly in need of magic.

Outside the window, I could see a crow sitting in the crook of an oak tree.

I hoped it was Clarence.

It is a nice thing to believe that a crow is watching over you.

"So," said Reverend Obertask.

"So," I said. "Here is your pipe."

Reverend Obertask reached forward and took the pipe from my hand very gently. "Thank you," he said. "You didn't tell me your name."

"Louisiana Elefante."

It was the first time I had said that name since I had learned the truth about myself, and I must say that the words felt strange in my mouth – heavy and dark.

"Are you of Spanish extraction?" said Reverend Obertask.

"I have absolutely no idea," I said. "The sad fact is that my parents are entirely unknown to me."

It was strange to say those words, too. Always, before, my parents had been crystal clear in my mind – golden, shimmery, beautiful. But now when I thought of them, no image appeared. There was nothing but darkness, and that was sad, because before there had been so much brightness.

"I used to believe that my parents were trapeze artists known as the Flying Elefantes," I said to Reverend Obertask. "But it turns out that I don't know who they were or what they did."

Oh, I felt hollow inside.

Reverend Obertask nodded. He said, "I see." His chair creaked once, twice, and then the office was very quiet. I could see dust motes dancing around joyfully in the air.

What do dust motes have to be so happy about?

Reverend Obertask cleared his throat. He said, "So you were adopted, I presume?"

"It is a long and tragic story full of dark alleys and twists and turns and many unexpected happenings," I said. "And also curses. There are curses in the story."

"Curses," said Reverend Obertask.

"Yes," I said, "curses. Do you know much about curses?"

"I'm afraid I don't."

"But you're a minister," I said.

"I am," said Reverend Obertask. "However, my day-to-day interactions tend to deal more with everyday issues – the loss of hope, the combating of despair, the balm of forgiveness, the need to understand, the short tempers and distrustful natures of church organists. That sort of thing. It's not often that curses come up."

Out in the sanctuary, Miss Lulu started to play the organ. There was one huge crashing chord.

And then a long silence. And then came another huge crashing chord.

"I think she is frustrated sometimes," said Reverend Obertask. He smiled. "We all push against our limitations, don't we?"

I liked Reverend Obertask. I liked his smile. I liked his walrus face.

I thought that maybe he was the kind of person who would understand how it felt to sit in a motel room and stare at state-inappropriate curtains and know that you are all alone in the world.

"I have a curse upon my head," I told him. "And I was hoping that you could undo it."

"Alas," said Reverend Obertask, "I do not think that I can undo your curse. I wish that I could."

The sun went behind a cloud. I heard Clarence laughing. I heard Reverend Obertask breathing.

I stood there. I worked hard not to cry.

"Does this curse have to do with your parents?" said Reverend Obertask in a very quiet voice.

"It is a curse of sundering," I said, "so, yes, I suppose it does, because my parents left me in an alley, behind a dollar store."

Reverend Obertask nodded. He said, "What a terrible thing."

And it was a terrible thing, wasn't it?

It was a relief to hear somebody call it what it was: terrible.

"How could they do that?" I said. "How could they just leave me? What kind of people would do that? I don't understand."

Reverend Obertask shook his head. "I don't know," he said. "I don't understand either."

I have to say that Reverend Obertask was turning out to be something of a disappointment. He couldn't undo curses. He couldn't explain things.

From the sanctuary came the sound of Miss Lulu playing Bach on the organ. Or attempting to play Bach on the organ.

I did not understand how someone could play the organ so poorly, just as I did not understand how someone could have a seemingly lifetime supply of chocolate caramels and not share them.

There was so much I did not understand.

The sun came out from behind a cloud, and then it went back again – light, dark, light, dark.

I felt very sad.

I said, "I thought you would be able to help me. I thought you would have some kind of magic. On your door, it says that you dispense healing words."

"I can listen to you, Louisiana Elefante," said Reverend Obertask. "That is the only magic I have. Do you want to tell me the rest of your story?"

Reverend Obertask leant back in his chair, and it let out another creak. The dust motes danced around cheerfully. Miss Lulu continued to abuse Mr Bach.

"I have a question for you," I said.

"I will do my best to answer it," said Reverend Obertask.

"Do you know the story of Pinocchio?" I said.

"I do."

"Well, then you will know that Pinocchio gets separated from his father at the beginning of the book and spends the whole entire story separated from him until they meet up again in the belly of a whale."

"Yes," said Reverend Obertask.

"Will I spend the whole entire story of my life separated from the people I love?"

Reverend Obertask blinked. He said, "I don't know, Louisiana. I can't see into the future. I do think that, more often than not, love has a way of finding us."

I looked into Reverend Obertask's sad walrus face.

It was the second time that I had stood in Reverend Obertask's office and come to the realization that I was all on my own.

"It is a good and healing thing to tell your story," said Reverend Obertask. "So if you don't want to finish telling it to me, maybe you can find someone you trust to tell it to. Either way, I hope you will come and visit me again."

Poor ineffectual Reverend Obertask.

"Perhaps I will visit you again," I said, just to cheer him up.

He smiled at me.

And I smiled back at him, but I did not use all of my teeth because, oh, my heart was heavy.

Twenty-one

Burke and I were in the woods. We were sitting together under a tree, and Clarence was some-where where I could not see or hear him. But I knew he was there because he did not ever go too far away from Burke. And that was nice; that was comforting.

The sun was still shining and the world was still spinning and Reverend Obertask had not removed the curse from my head, but I felt differ-ent somehow.

I looked at Burke and said, "I am going to tell you what was in that terrible letter. And the first thing you need to know is that the Flying Elefantes do not exist."

The Flying Elefantes do not exist.

I hated that sentence. I hated it. But I had to say it.

"What do you mean they don't exist?" said Burke.

"I mean there were never any Flying Elefantes. I don't know who my parents were."

And then I went ahead and told him everything, all of it. I told him about young Granny and how her father had looked at her and then turned and walked away from her, and how that was when the curse truly began.

I told Burke about how Granny found me in the alley and picked me up. I told him that she was only someone who had found me and that I was not related to her at all. I told him that whoever Granny was, she was gone now, that she had left me and that I was alone in the world.

"Dang," said Burke when I was done. "Well, I guess the good news is that if she ain't no relation of yours, then the curse ain't your curse."

"What?" I said.

"It ain't your curse. It ain't on your head after all."

"I'm not cursed?" I said.

"I reckon not," said Burke. "Not the way I figure it."

I lay down in the grass. The world was suddenly spinning faster and faster.

Who was I without the Flying Elefantes?

Who was I without Granny?

And who was I without a curse upon my head?

I felt as light as air. I felt as insubstantial as the ghost of a cricket.

"Maybe I don't exist at all," I said to Burke.

"You surely do exist," said Burke. "I know it for a fact." He looked over at me, and then he stood up. He whistled, and Clarence came flying to him and landed on his shoulder.

"Stand up, Louisiana," said Burke.

"No," I said.

"You got to stand up."

"No," I said again.

The winds of fate had deposited me in the

alley of the dollar store, and then the winds of fate had picked me up and put me in the woods in Georgia, and that was where I was staying. I was never going to move again.

I was worse off even than Pinocchio, a wooden puppet who at least had a father who loved him and kept searching for him, not to mention a Blue Fairy who showed up from time to time.

I lay on the ground and Burke stood over me and Clarence opened and closed his wings again and again. The sun came beating down through the trees and landed on Burke's arm and lit up Clarence's feathers.

The world was beautiful.

It surprised me, how beautiful it kept on insisting on being. In spite of all the lies, it was beautiful. In her letter, "Granny" said that I had smiled at her in the alley of the dollar store. Was that true?

"Louisiana?" said Burke.

"What?" I said.

"Don't you want to go and find your granny?"

"No," I said. "I don't think so. I don't know what I want. I don't know who I am."

"OK," said Burke. "All right. We'll figure this out. Didn't you say you had a dog and a cat and friends in Florida?"

Buddy. Archie. Raymie. Beverly.

"Yes," I said.

"Didn't you say Florida was where you belonged?"

"Yes," I said.

"All right, then," said Burke. "You need to go home."

Burke was right. I needed to go home.

I stood up. I said, "What direction is Florida, again?"

Burke rolled his eyes. He said, "I'll help you, all right? I'll go with you. Me and Clarence both. We need us a map and a bus schedule, and we'll go to Florida."

First we went to the Good Night, Sleep Tight to collect my belongings, but the door to Room 102 was locked, and when we went into the motel reception, Bernice told Burke to get out.

"You thief," she said. "Leave here immediately."

"I'll wait on you outside, Louisiana," said Burke.

Bernice's hair was still in curlers.

My goodness, I was tired of seeing those curlers. I was tired of seeing Bernice, too.

"What do you want?" she said to me.

"I am here to collect my belongings," I said.

"No," said Bernice. "Your grandmother has absconded, and I do not want to hear whatever hard-luck story you might have about that. I don't want to hear any of it. You will get your suitcase when the bill is paid, and the bill will only be paid when you have sung at the funeral."

I stared at Bernice's head. I concentrated on one curler in particular, and stared at it just as hard as I could. I stared death rays into that curler!

"I'm not afraid of you," I said.

"Good," said Bernice. "I'm not afraid of you, either. I'm tired of people taking advantage of my good nature."

I wondered what good nature she was talking about.

"The funeral is at noon tomorrow," she said.

Everything I owned was in that suitcase, and I did not have the energy for a battle of the wills.

"Fine," I said. "I will sing at the funeral."

"You bet you will," said Bernice. "Be here at eleven thirty tomorrow morning."

"OK," I said. "And maybe as an extra-special surprise for me, you will actually remove the curlers from your hair."

I walked out of the office, and Burke was waiting for me.

He had got me peanuts from the machine!

"I can't leave yet," I said. "I have to sing at the funeral tomorrow or else I can't get my suitcase back. And I can't leave my suitcase behind, because I have already left too many things behind."

"That works out fine," said Burke. "It'll give us time to plan out the whole thing. You can stay at my house tonight and tomorrow night, and we can leave early on Saturday morning."

I said, "Yes, that is exactly what we will do. We will leave."

I felt a sudden wave of weariness.

My goodness, I was tired of leaving places.

For someone who did not actually have a curse of sundering on her head, it seemed to me that I was involved in quite a bit of sundering.

Twenty-two

When we got back to the pink house in the woods, it smelled sweet again, because Betty Allen was baking another one of her seventeen cakes. This one was pineapple upside-down.

"I have never in my life had a pineapple upside-down cake," I said to Betty Allen.

"Well, we will have to rectify that, I am sure," said Betty Allen. "In the meantime, I would like it if Burke Allen explained to me why he wasn't in school today."

"I was helping Louisiana," said Burke.

"You can't keep skipping school, Burke," said

Betty Allen. "After a time, it will catch up with you, and you will find that life has closed its doors to you. You don't want life to close its doors to you, do you?"

"No, ma'am," said Burke. He looked down at his feet.

"Open doors," said Betty Allen. "That is what we want – doors that are open to us." She put her hand on Burke's head and left it there a minute, and then she turned to me. "Sweetie," she said, "is that the same dress you had on yesterday?"

"It is," I said. "My other dresses are in my luggage, and my luggage is currently unavailable to me."

"Why is your luggage currently unavailable to you?"

"Many terrible and complicated things have happened," I said.

"Well, what are they?"

I stood in the sweet-smelling house and looked into Betty Allen's gentle face. She looked back at me.

I wanted to tell her that I didn't even know

who I was. I wanted to tell her that I had been left. I wanted to tell her that she reminded me of the Blue Fairy.

What I said was, "Have you ever read the story of Pinocchio?"

Burke gave me a shove. He said, "Louisiana's granny ain't feeling good. Can Louisiana stay here with us?"

"What is wrong with your granny?" said Betty Allen.

"She is having tooth problems," I said. "And she needs some time to recuperate. She is extremely unwell. She is also a liar."

Burke gave me another little shove. He said, "Can Louisiana stay or not?"

"Well, for heaven's sake, Burke," said Betty Allen. "Of course Louisiana can stay." She kept her eyes on me. She gave me a very serious look, and then she smiled the most beautiful smile and reached out her hand and placed it on the top of my head just the same as she had done with Burke. It felt nice.

"Thank you, Mama," said Burke.

"Thank you, Mrs Allen," I said.

"Why don't you two go and wash your hands," said Betty Allen. "Supper will be ready soon."

At the dinner table that night, I sat next to Grandfather Burke.

He said, "Looka here. There she is. Setting right at the table, as pretty as you please. You need you a phone book to set on so as you can reach the table?"

"Don't pick on her, Grandpap," said Burke.

"Pick on her? I ain't picking on her. I'm glad to see her is all." He winked at me.

"Daddy," said Burke's father, "you let her alone now. Let her eat."

The dinner was fried chicken and green beans and mashed potatoes, and I ate everything set before me and it was all very good, but truly I wasn't even certain that I was there.

I kept imagining the dark alley of the Louisiana Dollar Store.

I kept hearing Burke say, "The curse ain't your curse."

I kept seeing Betty Allen smile at me.

There was vanilla ice cream with chocolate sauce for dessert. We each had our own little cut-glass bowl. There were peanuts sprinkled on top of the chocolate sauce.

I ate all my ice cream. I scraped the bowl with my spoon, and then Grandfather Burke slid his bowl of ice cream over so that it was sitting right in front of me.

I looked down at Grandfather Burke's bowl.

The glass was twinkling in the light. It looked very pretty. It was dark outside, and there were lights on inside and the bowl was catching all the light, and everybody was around the table and the bowl was full of ice cream and chocolate sauce and peanuts, and I felt as if I was right on the verge of understanding something.

And then Grandfather Burke said, "That's for you, doodlebug."

I stared down at the beautiful bowl, and I started to cry.

"Why are you crying?" he said.

I shook my head.

"Leave her alone, Grandpap," said Burke.

"I ain't done nothing to her except to give her my dessert."

I was crying too hard to pick up my spoon, and that is something that has never happened to me before.

"What ails her?" said the grandfather.

"She misses her granny," said Burke.

"I do not miss my granny!" I said.

Grandfather Burke took hold of my hand. In a very gentle voice, he said, "Go on and eat it, darling. Take what is offered to you."

Holding on to his horse hoof gave me some courage and comfort, and after a while, I stopped crying and picked up my spoon.

"There you go, honey," said Betty Allen.

I ate the whole bowl of ice cream without once letting go of Grandfather Burke's hand.

"That's the way to do it," he said. "That's just right."

The peanuts on top of the sundae were particularly good.

The house smelled like pineapple upside-down cake.

Well, the whole world was upside down.

But it was still spinning.

Wasn't it?

Twenty-three

In the morning, Burke went to school. He said he would find the atlas and tear out the map of Florida and locate Lister and figure out exactly how to get there.

And Betty Allen washed my dress for me, which was very nice and thoughtful of her.

At eleven thirty sharp, I walked into the Good Night, Sleep Tight and turned myself over to Bernice, who did not have her hair in curlers.

You can imagine my surprise. I almost didn't recognize her.

She was wearing a shiny black dress, and her

hair wasn't very curly when you considered how much time it had spent in curlers. Mostly, Bernice looked annoyed.

Well, I was annoyed too. I wanted my suit-case back. I wanted to go home, even though I felt somewhat sad about sundering myself from Betty Allen and Burke Allen, and also from the grandfather Burke Allen, who was very good about sharing his food with me.

We drove to the Lonely Shepherd Church in Bernice's green Buick Skylark. Bernice did not speak to me, and I did not speak to her. Bernice and I were never going to be friends, and that was just fine with me. Actually, I hoped that I never had to see her again in my life.

I hoped that I never had to see Miss Lulu again either.

"You are going to sing twice," Miss Lulu said to me when we arrived at the church. She held up two fingers. "At the beginning of the funeral and again at the end. You are going to sing the same song both times."

The song was "Amazing Grace", and it is a

song that I have sung a hundred thousand times before because it is what people always want sung at funerals and I have sung at a hundred thousand funerals because it was a good way for that granny person to make some money.

"Here are the words," said Miss Lulu, "if you would like to review them." She handed me a piece of sheet music.

I did not take it from her.

"I know the words," I said.

She sighed, and the sigh smelled like caramel. You would think that eating all that chocolate would rot her teeth out. I hoped it did.

"I wonder if this child takes her responsibility here seriously," Miss Lulu said to Bernice.

"I assure you she does," said Bernice. She gave me a deadly look.

"Well, let me tell you something," said Miss Lulu. "I discovered her sneaking around Reverend Obertask's office yesterday with his *pipe* in her hand. Can you imagine?"

"She's capable of anything," said Bernice. "Her grandmother has disappeared, you know.

Vanished. Left the child here on her own. As far as I can tell, she is staying with the Allens, and as you are well aware, that Burke Allen is nothing but a truant and vandal, and he will certainly do nothing to further this child's moral education."

The two of them went on talking as if I wasn't even standing there.

Miss Lulu's curls bounced with every word she said.

Bernice's fake curls, however, did not move at all.

The church was filling up with people. And then Reverend Obertask appeared and said to me, "Louisiana Elefante, it is a delight to gaze upon your winsome face once again."

Miss Lulu snorted.

Reverend Obertask put a comforting hand on my shoulder. He said, "Let's get this show on the road."

"We will begin with the child singing," said Miss Lulu.

"Just as it should be," said Reverend Obertask. "Just exactly as it should be."

. . .

The light came in through the stained-glass windows. Bernice went and sat down, and Miss Lulu started to play the organ, and I stood up there and sang.

Miss Lulu's playing was terrible, of course.

But it was just not possible for me to sing without putting my whole heart into it. "You have a gift, Louisiana, and the more of yourself you put into the song, the more powerful – the more truthful – the song becomes."

That is what "Granny" said to me.

As if that woman knew anything about the truth.

What a liar she was. She was nothing but a liar. Maybe I wasn't found in an alley at all. Who could say? And speaking of alleys, what kind of people put their baby on top of a pile of cardboard boxes in a dark alley?

It was terrible. Just as Reverend Obertask had said. My parents were terrible. No real mother would ever leave her baby in an alley. Why, Betty

Allen would never do such a thing to Burke Allen in a million, trillion years.

Oh, it made me mad to think about it – all of it.

But even though I was mad, I put myself into the song.

I put every bit of myself into it.

There was a rustling out in the pews. It was the sound of people pulling tissues out of their pockets and their purses. They were all crying, and that was good. I wanted them to cry.

I put even more of myself in the song.

And then I saw something truly terrible.

Sitting right there in the very front row was Mrs Ivy from the dentist's office. Her lips were in a straight line, and she was pulling a piece of paper out of her purse. Oh, my goodness, it was the bill for teeth removal! She was waving it in the air!

And then I noticed that Dr Fox was sitting right next to Mrs Ivy. His little round glasses were winking in the light. He was wearing his dental coat. There was still a spot of blood on it. It seemed like a very inappropriate thing to wear to a funeral.

The room tilted sideways, and then it righted

itself again. My goodness, the church building was like a ship on stormy waters.

I kept singing.

And then I saw her – I saw "Granny". I couldn't believe it. She was sitting right behind Dr Fox. She was wearing her fur coat, and she was smiling at me, using all of her teeth. Was she back already from fighting the curse? How did she manage to recover her teeth? Was there no end to her powers?

Way at the back of the church, somebody went floating by in a flying-trapeze kind of outfit, which is also not the kind of thing you should wear to a funeral. But maybe the spangly outfit was just something I imagined because it was there – a flash of light – and then it was gone.

When I looked away from the glittery light and back at "Granny", she was still smiling at me. She was sitting up very tall, reminding me to stand up straight, to project my heart into the world.

I shook my head.

The sanctuary was tilting terribly again. Everything was sliding to one side. I stopped singing.

And then Miss Lulu stopped playing the organ, which was a relief.

Everything was silent as silent could be.

And that is when Clarence flew into the Good Shepherd, his dark feathers shining like a light.

Clarence had come looking for me.

It was so quiet in the church that you could hear the flapping of his wings.

It sounded like the beating of a heart.

"Granny" smiled at me. She said, "Provisions have been made, Louisiana."

At least I think that is what she said.

All I know for certain is that the church tipped again, and this time I tipped with it.

Twenty-four

I woke up in Reverend Obertask's office. I was on the floor, and my head was on a pillow made out of a scratchy tweed jacket.

Reverend Obertask was sitting at his desk, staring down at me.

"Ah," he said. "There you are."

"Here I am," I said.

"You fainted."

The sun was shining in through Reverend Obertask's window and landing right on his head so that he looked like a walrus in a religious painting. Not that I had ever seen a walrus in a religious painting. Camels, yes. And also horses. And sometimes dogs. And angels, of course. There are always angels in religious paintings. You don't see that many angels in real life, though.

Reverend Obertask smiled at me.

"Mourners faint at funerals," he said. "It's a common occurrence. But you are the first musician I've ever known to faint mid-song. Miss Lulu is supremely agitated, of course. She likes for things to go a certain way, a predictable way."

Well, I understood that feeling.

Not that I have ever experienced things going a predictable way.

I closed my eyes. I saw "Granny" smiling with all of her teeth. I saw Mrs Ivy waving the bill. I saw Dr Fox in his bloody jacket.

And then I saw Clarence's wings, dark and shiny, beating out the rhythm of a heart.

I opened my eyes and looked at Reverend Obertask. "Was there a crow in church?"

"Not to my knowledge."

"Oh," I said. "What about a dentist? Did you see a dentist?"

"I did not," said Reverend Obertask. "Although I must say that they are a little more difficult to identify at a glance."

"Did you see anyone wearing a fur coat?"

"No crows, no dentists, no fur coats," said Reverend Obertask. He smiled at me again.

I said, "I don't know who I am. I only know that I am not who I thought I was."

Reverend Obertask nodded his big head. "That is a problem we all face sooner or later, I suppose."

From out in the church, there came the crashing sound of Miss Lulu on the organ.

Reverend Obertask stood up. "Clearly Miss Lulu is becoming impatient," he said. "There is still a funeral to run. Why don't you rest? I'll drive you home when this is all over. We can talk things through."

I closed my eyes.

Reverend Obertask the walrus was going to drive me home.

I wondered where that was – home.

"Provisions have been made." That is what the

Granny mirage had said to me. Or that was what I had heard.

And then, before I knew it, I was asleep. Because I was just so very, very tired.

Reverend Obertask took me to the Allens' house. You could smell the cake baking when we were still out in the woods, before the pink house even came into view.

Reverend Obertask knocked on the back door, and Betty Allen opened it and said, "What in the world?" She opened her arms to me, and I walked right into them. Betty Allen held me tight for a minute, and then she let me go.

"There was a little mishap at the funeral," said Reverend Obertask. "My, but it smells wonderful in here."

Betty Allen blushed. "I am the official baker for the carnival," she said.

"Yes, indeed," said Reverend Obertask. "That is why it's called the World-Famous Betty Allen Cake Raffle. What particular cake am I smelling now?"

"That is my pound cake," said Betty Allen. "It is not a fancy cake, but it is very, very good. It is my great-grandmother's recipe."

"It smells divine," said Reverend Obertask.

"I would like to win a pound cake in the World-Famous Betty Allen Cake Raffle," I said.

"Oh, honey," said Betty Allen.

"How would you feel about Mrs Allen and myself having a private word?" said Reverend Obertask to me.

"Burke should be home from school any minute now," said Betty Allen. "You could wait for him outside."

I went out the back door and stood in the driveway and listened to Reverend Obertask say, "I am very worried about this child."

And Betty Allen said back to him, "I am worried too."

I could tell that the conversation between Reverend Obertask and Betty Allen was going to be extremely sad, and I just didn't think my heart could bear to listen. I walked away from them, down to the end of the driveway. I stood and looked out at the woods.

I whistled for Clarence the same way Burke did – two low whistles and then one high one.

But Clarence didn't come.

I sat down on the ground.

On the drive back from the funeral, I had told Reverend Obertask my story. Or most of my story. I did not tell him that "Granny" was gone, because I did not want Reverend Obertask to contact the authorities. In any case, I started with Elf Ear, Nebraska, and the stage and the sundering that occurred there. I told him about the letter from the fake granny and how it told the story of a magician walking away from his daughter without saying anything to her at all, and also the story of the Louisiana Dollar Store and the dark alley and the flowered blanket and what was inside it – which was me.

I told him about Dr Fox pulling every last one of "Granny's" teeth and me lying to Mrs Ivy about the bill. I told him about the Good Night, Sleep Tight and how it had a vending machine in the foyer with everything you could ever want inside of it, and also how there was a stuffed alligator in the lobby who was very ferocious-looking. I told him that there had been curtains with palm trees all over them in Room 102 and how it was wrong for palm trees to be on curtains in Georgia.

I told him that Bernice was holding my suitcase for ransom and that I would probably never see it again. I told him how I had asked Burke Allen for one tinned-meat sandwich and he had given me two. I told him that Betty Allen was making seventeen cakes – seventeen! – and that the grandfather Burke Allen had given me his bowl of ice cream with chocolate sauce and peanuts on top of it and that he had held my hand while I ate it.

I told him about Beverly and Raymie. I told him about Buddy the one-eyed dog and how the three of us had rescued him together. I told him about Archie, King of the Cats, and how, once, he had found his way back to me. I told him about the time I almost drowned and that the Blue Fairy had shown up underwater, smiling at me and holding out her arms, and that part of me wanted to go with her, deeper into the pond.

I told him that the operator on the phone in his office had told me that there were no listings for Tapinski and too many listings for Clarke with an *e*, and no Raymie Clarke at all, and how could that be?

And speaking of how things could be, I asked him again how anybody could leave a baby in an alley.

How could that be?

How could it?

Reverend Obertask stared straight ahead at the road the whole time I was talking.

And here was the surprising thing: he cried.

I talked and he kept his eyes on the road, and I watched one tear and then another tear creep down his sad walrus face and disappear into his whiskers.

When we got to the Good Night, Sleep Tight, I said to Reverend Obertask, "I want to get my suitcase back from Bernice, and I want to go to the Allens' house because Granny is still unwell and needs to sleep a healing sleep."

Reverend Obertask said, "Please wait here, Louisiana."

He went into the motel reception, and a few minutes later, he came walking out with my suitcase. The suitcase looked very small in his big hand.

When he got back into the car, Reverend Obertask turned to me and said, "I want you to know something, Louisiana. We all, at some point, have to decide who we want to be in this world. It is a decision we make for ourselves. You are being forced to make this decision at an early age, but that does not mean that you cannot do it well and wisely. I believe you can. I have great faith in you. You decide. You decide who you are, Louisiana. Do you understand?"

I told him that I did understand.

Even though I wasn't certain that I did.

"And another thing," he said. "You will never understand why your parents left you in that alley. It is impossible to understand. But it may be necessary for you to forgive them, for your own sake, without ever truly understanding what they did. OK?"

His face was so serious and sad that I said, "Yes, Reverend Obertask. I understand."

But I didn't understand. How could I forgive people who had never shown me any kindness? How could I forgive people who had left me behind without loving me at all?

And so it came to pass that I found myself sitting at the end of a long driveway in front of a pink house that smelled like cake, thinking about forgiveness and who I wanted to be in this world.

Twenty-five

I sat there until Burke Allen came walking out of the woods with Clarence sitting on his shoulder.

"Hey," said Burke. "Hey, Louisiana. Guess what? I got the whole thing planned out. I know just where to go and what bus to get on and the whole thing."

And just as he said that, I heard Reverend Obertask say my name.

"Louisiana," he said.

I turned and looked behind me, and lo and behold, I saw the walrus and the Blue Fairy standing together at the top of the driveway. And even though Pinocchio does not encounter a walrus on his journey, Reverend Obertask and Betty Allen standing there together looked like something out of Pinocchio's story come to life.

Reverend Obertask waved at me, and then he came walking down the driveway and took hold of my hand. He said, "Thank you for talking with me, Louisiana."

I said, "You are welcome."

And then Betty Allen said my name.

"Louisiana Elefante," she called out, "I wonder if you would like to come and help me bake the last cake, which is a marble cake."

"Me?" I said.

"Yes, you, honey."

"Is a marble cake a cake with surprise marbles in it?" I said.

"There's a recipe," said Betty Allen. "The two of us will follow it together."

"Why don't you go on up there and help her?" said Reverend Obertask. "I'll get your suitcase out of the car."

Clarence flapped his wings and took off from Burke's shoulder and flew away.

Reverend Obertask let go of my hand.

"Go on, Louisiana," said Burke. "I'll wait for you."

The kitchen in the pink house was painted a bright yellow, and being in that room with Betty Allen was like standing inside of the sun.

"Now, what I am going to have you do is measure out the flour and the baking powder and the salt – all the dry ingredients, basically," said Betty Allen.

I said, "I've never made any kind of cake before."

"Never, ever?" said Betty Allen.

"No," I said. "My granny does not believe in baking."

Betty Allen put her hands on her hips. "Well, for heaven's sake. What does she believe in?"

That was a good question.

I considered it.

"Singing," I said finally. "She believes in me singing."

Betty Allen nodded. "Reverend Obertask did say that you have a beautiful voice. Now, here is the flour and salt and what-have-you, and also a few bowls and measuring cups and spoons, and I will just put you to work on this counter over here."

I measured the flour and the salt and the baking powder, and the whole time, Betty Allen was standing at the counter opposite me humming under her breath.

It was warm in the kitchen, and the yellow walls were so bright and Betty Allen's humming was so musical that I started to think that maybe things weren't as tragic as they seemed.

Betty Allen said, "Maybe when we have baked this cake, we will take a big old piece of it to your granny at the Good Night, Sleep Tight."

"That is not at all necessary," I said very, very quickly.

"Your granny doesn't like cake?" said Betty Allen.

"Her teeth hurt too much to eat," I said. "It is very difficult to eat cake when you are toothless.

The world in general becomes a difficult place without teeth."

"Oh," said Betty Allen. "I see." She went back to humming.

We put everything together into one big bowl – the wet ingredients and the dry ingredients – and mixed it all together with the electric mixer and then poured half of it into a cake tin.

"There," said Betty Allen. "Now we will add the cocoa powder to the rest of the batter and swirl it all around. That's the marbling part. Maybe you want to do that?"

She stood over me. She put her hands on my shoulders and said, "Just pour it on there and swirl."

I poured. I swirled.

"That's right," said Betty Allen. "Make it as swirly as you want."

When I was done, Betty Allen kept her hands on my shoulders, and we both stared together down at the cake. She said, "Louisiana, you can trust me. You can tell me the truth. Is your granny gone?"

I didn't answer her. I couldn't answer her.

I also couldn't keep myself from crying.

And once I started crying, I couldn't stop.

I stood there in the yellow kitchen in the pink house, and I cried and cried. I cried because Granny was truly and for ever gone, and somehow I knew that she was not coming back. I cried because I was alone. I cried because the curse was not my curse. I cried, and my tears of sadness and despair and hope and anger fell directly into the marble cake that had no marbles.

Betty Allen said, "We would be happy to help you try to find your granny, honey. But you can stay with us for as long as you need to. You can have a home with us, if that's what you want."

It was such a simple sentence.

Why did it sound so beautiful and impossible?

"Think about it," said Betty Allen. "I know Emma Stonehill over in Family Services. I could talk to her. Reverend Obertask could talk to her too. We could find a way to make it work, honey."

She picked up the cake tin and turned away from me and opened the oven door. And when the marble cake was inside the oven and the door was closed, Betty Allen clapped her hands together as if she had just performed a magic trick.

"Now," she said, "run on out there and look for Burke. I know he's waiting for you. And, honey, we would all love to have you stay here with us and be a part of our family, but it is your decision entirely."

It was my decision. Entirely.

I went outside, and Burke was there.

He looked at me, and, my goodness, his eyes were bright, and it occurred to me that they were probably so bright because he had never had to ask himself who he was or where he belonged or who he wanted to be. He was Burke Allen, who was the son of Burke Allen, who was the son of Burke Allen, on and on. Infinitely.

"Do you still want to go to Florida?" said Burke.

"I don't know," I told him. "I don't know what I want to do."

He nodded.

He whistled for Clarence.

And then Burke said, "Come on and follow me."

Twenty-six

"When I can't think what to do, or when I need to solve a really hard problem, what I do is climb up high, up to the top of that Good Night sign," said Burke.

"Well, I am not climbing up to the top of that sign," I said. "Because as I told you before, I am afraid of heights."

"We don't have to go to the top of the sign," said Burke. "Just to the top of a tree. Sitting in a tree and looking up can help you figure things out."

Well, I didn't have any more strength to argue with him.

And in addition, I didn't know who I was. For all I knew, I was somebody who was *not* afraid of heights. My goodness, it was possible.

I followed Burke to the big oak tree beside the Good Night, Sleep Tight. He climbed up into the crook of it, and then he stood there and looked down at me. "All you have to do is give me your hand, Louisiana," he said. "I'll go on ahead of you, and I'll keep holding out my hand to you, all right?"

"Go ahead," I said.

Clarence was sitting on a branch, watching both of us.

"This here is the first step," said Burke. "This is where you start. Come on. You have to do the first part on your own. Grab hold of the tree."

I walked closer to the tree.

Clarence laughed.

"Grab hold of that branch right there," said Burke.

I took hold of the branch. It was rough and warm.

"Good," said Burke. "Now, go on and pull yourself up just a bit."

I pulled myself up.

Burke smiled at me. He went up higher in the tree.

"Come on, now," he said. He held out his hand.

Well, I was off the ground and in the tree, and I just didn't think I was interested in going much further. The person I used to call Granny had always told me that I was "overly cautious physically". And I suppose I was.

But maybe I didn't have to be.

Maybe it was like Reverend Obertask had said: I could decide who I wanted to be.

Burke said, "Louisiana, if you take my hand and come up higher, I will go and get you anything you want out of that old vending machine."

And that is always the problem with me, isn't it?

I cannot keep from wanting things.

"I want peanuts," I said.

"All right," said Burke. He stuck his hand out further.

"And an Oh Henry! bar."

"OK," he said.

"Two Oh Henry! bars."

"I'll get you everything you want," he said.

I took Burke's hand. It felt rough and warm, the same as the tree branch.

"Come on," said Burke. "I've got hold of you. Put your foot right there. Don't look down."

I put my foot where he told me to. I kept hold of his hand. I did not look down. And bit by bit, we climbed to the top of the tree.

It is a wondrous thing to be at the top of a tree!

Particularly when you have two Oh Henry! bars to eat. And a bag of peanuts.

When we got to the top, Burke left me and climbed back down to go to the vending machine.

I stayed and held on to the branch. I looked down and guess what?

I did not feel afraid. I truly did not. Maybe it was because Clarence was on the branch next to me, or maybe it was just because I was done with being afraid. Or who knows? Maybe I had never been afraid of heights to begin with. Maybe it was just one more lie that "Granny" had told me about myself.

I don't know.

But I do know that I ate both chocolate bars and all the peanuts. Burke and Clarence were beside me, and even though the light was fading, I was happy.

The three of us watched together as the sky turned into a purple kind of blue.

"Look," said Burke. "You can see the stars now."

It got darker and the stars got brighter, and I still felt happy, so I started to sing. I sang a song about sitting in a tree with a boy and a crow, looking up at the stars.

It was a happy song. I put an Oh Henry! bar into it. And also peanuts and a marble cake. I did not add curses or dark alleys. I put only happy things in the song, and it made me happy to sing it.

"Dang," said Burke when I was done. "That's a good song."

At least I knew that about myself. At least I knew I was somebody who could sing.

That was something Granny had given me.

She had given me a lot, I suppose.

"Look right there," I said to Burke. "That's the Pinocchio constellation."

"Where?" said Burke.

"That one right there. See? That is the face, and that is the long nose of someone telling a lie."

"Shoot, Louisiana," said Burke. "That constellation is called the Big Dipper. Grandpap showed me that one for ever ago. See how it looks like a big old scoop? And that's the handle to it, right there. It ain't a nose. It's a handle. And over there is the North Star. That's the one you want to look for when you're lost in the woods, because then you know what direction north is, and then you ain't lost any more."

"Oh," I said.

I stared up at the North Star. I could not imagine not being lost.

"We should probably head on back so they don't come looking for us," said Burke. "You want me to help you? With the climbing down?"

"No," I said. "I can do it. You go ahead of me and I'll follow you."

"All right," said Burke.

"Have you ever had marble cake?" I asked Burke as we went down the tree.

"I have had all of them cakes that Mama makes," he said. "I have had every one of them. They're all good."

"Your mother figured out that Granny is gone," I said when we were both back on the ground.

Burke turned to me.

"And she told me that I could stay with you," I said. "That I could live with your family."

"That means you ain't going to go back to Florida, then?"

"I don't know what I'm going to do," I said. "Do you want me to stay?"

Burke shrugged. He said, "I think it would be all right if you stayed. I think it would be great if you stayed." He shrugged again. "But I ain't going to tell you what to do."

I nodded. I said, "Show me again which star is the North Star."

Burke pointed. "That one. Right there."

"Thank you," I said.

It seems like a good thing to know the star that can keep you from being lost in this world.

Twenty-seven

We all went to the carnival – me and Burke and Betty Allen and the father Burke and the grand-father Burke. And I still had not made up my mind whether I would stay or whether I would leave. I just could not decide.

But the good news is that the World-Famous Betty Allen Cake Raffle was set up on the lawn in front of the Lost Shepherd Church. The cakes were arranged end to end on a long table, and they were beautiful to behold.

There was a large glass fishbowl on the table too, and every time somebody bought a raffle ticket, Betty Allen ripped the ticket in half and put one half into the bowl and handed the other half back to the person who hoped to win a cake.

The piano had been rolled out from the social hall, and Miss Lulu was playing what she must have thought was an appropriate cake raffling song. It occurred to me that no matter what I did, I just could not escape from Miss Lulu and her attempts at making music.

It cost a dollar for every ticket, and Burke Allen the grandfather gave me five dollars so I could purchase five tickets because I really, really wanted to win a cake.

"I would buy you all them cakes, doodlebug," said Grandfather Burke. "I would buy you every last one of them. You don't even got to throw your tiny hat into the ring. All you got to do is say the word and I will buy 'em all up for you."

But I wanted to enter the raffle.

I wanted to throw my tiny hat into the ring.

I wanted to take my chances.

Miss Lulu continued to play music – pounding away at what sounded to me like a cake raffle dirge – until all the tickets were sold and then Betty Allen said, "We have seventeen cakes, ladies and gentlemen. And I will call seventeen winning numbers."

People applauded, and I clapped too. And then I looked down at my tickets. Were they winning tickets? I could not tell. I studied them very carefully.

Betty Allen cleared her throat. Miss Lulu played a dramatic piano roll.

Betty Allen said, "The first winner is two fifty-six."

Well, I did not have ticket number 256. I went through my five tickets several times just to make sure. A very large lady in a purple dress shouted, "That's me! That's me! I have won a cake!" And she moved up to the table to select her cake while Miss Lulu played another dramatic roll on the piano, and everybody applauded.

And then we started all over again. Betty Allen put her hand into the fishbowl. Miss Lulu played some piano, and then Betty Allen pulled out a ticket and called out a number, and it was not my number.

Pretty soon, we had made it through almost all the cakes. There was just one left and it was the pineapple upside-down cake, and even though I would have been very happy to win it, I have to say that the pineapple rings on the top of it seemed the tiniest bit desperate. There is something very sad about pineapple rings.

I looked up at Grandfather Burke. He was studying me with a serious look on his face. And then I looked over at Betty Allen. She was holding the bowl with the numbers in it, and she was watching me too.

I smiled at Betty Allen, and she smiled back at me. The light was shining off the fishbowl in a very beautiful way. Betty Allen put the bowl back on the table and reached her hand in and pulled out the last ticket. She did not once take her eyes off me.

I thought, *I have won! I have won the last cake!*

The fishbowl was all lit up with numbers and light. It really was a beautiful fishbowl.

And then I remembered the little glass bowls that Betty Allen had used for the ice-cream sundaes.

I remembered sitting at the glass-topped table with all of the Allens. I remembered Grandfather Burke sliding his bowl over to me and saying, "That's for you, doodlebug. Take what is offered to you."

And I knew what I wanted to do.

I knew who I wanted to be.

I wanted to be the person who sat at that table.

I wanted to stay.

Betty Allen cleared her throat. She called out the last winning number.

And guess what?

It was not my number. I did not win a cake.

But I did not care.

I was staying.

Twenty-eight

And so here I am, Granny, almost at the end of the story.

Imagine how surprised I am to find that you are the one I am writing it for.

And speaking of surprise, you will not be surprised to learn that Reverend Obertask is better at dealing with telephone operators than I am.

I stood beside him in his office at the Good Shepherd Church while he talked to all the wrong Clarkes and then to the right Clarke – Raymie's mother.

And then, finally, Reverend Obertask said,

"Hello, Raymie Clarke. There is someone here who needs to speak to you," and he handed the phone to me.

And the very first thing Raymie said to me was that Archie was there with her!

She said he showed up at the back door and yowled until they let him in, and he has stayed there. He hasn't left the house at all. And Raymie believed that I would show up again too.

"When are you coming back?" said Raymie.

I had to tell her that you were gone, Granny. And that you were not my granny to begin with, and that you had picked me up in an alley, and that my parents were not the Flying Elefantes and that my real parents were unknown to me, and that I was not, after all, afraid of heights. I told her everything.

And then I had to tell her I was staying in Georgia.

"What do you mean, staying?" said Raymie.

"I mean I am going to live here with the Allen family."

"But what about us?" said Raymie.

I started to cry then.

The sun was shining into Reverend Obertask's office. It was lighting up his walrus whiskers and the perpetually joyous dust motes.

And a long way away in Florida, Raymie was crying too. I could hear her.

Reverend Obertask cleared his throat. He said, "You know, people in Florida visit people in Georgia quite frequently."

I took a deep breath. I said to Raymie, "You could come see me. All of you could come see me. I am only one state away."

They came to visit a week later.

Mrs Clarke drove Raymie and Beverly and Buddy and Archie over the Florida–Georgia state line. She said that it was like being in charge of a travelling circus to have all of them in one car, but they came.

And Burke Allen and Betty Allen and I have gone to visit Beverly and Raymie and Buddy in Florida.

Archie, King of the Cats, goes back and forth. Sometimes he stays with me, and sometimes he stays with Raymie, because he is a cat and he does what he wants to do.

Clarence the crow is starting to trust me. He comes when I whistle. He has not yet landed upon my shoulder. But he will, Granny. He will.

I have respected your wishes. I have not come searching for you. But I have crossed the Florida–Georgia state line many, many times since we last spoke, and I look for you every time I cross over. I know that you will not be there, but I look anyway.

And I dream about you.

In my dream, you are standing in front of the vending machine from the Good Night, Sleep Tight, and you are smiling at me, using all of your teeth. You say, "Select anything you want, darling. Provisions have been made. Provisions have been made."

I am so happy when you show up in my dreams and say those words to me.

Thank you for picking me up in the alley of the Louisiana Dollar Store.

Thank you for teaching me to sing.

I don't know if you made it to Elf Ear or not.

But I want you to know that there is no curse of sundering upon my head.

I love you, Granny.

I forgive you.

Kate DiCamillo is the beloved author of many books for young readers, including two Newbery Medal winners: *The Tale of Despereaux* and *Flora & Ulysses: The Illuminated Adventures*. She grew up in Florida and moved to Minnesota in her twenties, where homesickness and a bitter winter led her to write her first published novel, *Because of Winn-Dixie*. It was named a Newbery Honor Book and she followed it with many other award-winning novels, among them *The Tiger Rising*, *The Miraculous Journey of Edward Tulane* and *The Magician's Elephant*. Her novel *Raymie Nightingale* tells the story of Louisiana Elefante's best friend Raymie, and is where Louisiana makes her first appearance.

Kate was selected to be the US National Ambassador for Young People's Literature 2014–2015. Of that mission, and on the power of stories, she says, "When we read together, we connect. Together, we see the world. Together, we see one another." Kate now lives in Minneapolis. Visit her website for more information about her books:

www.KateDiCamilloStoriesConnectUs.com

Also by
KATE DiCAMILLO

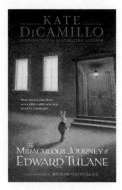

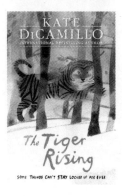

"DiCamillo is a star of the children's publishing world." *The New York Times*

Meet Raymie, Louisiana and Beverly in Kate DiCamillo's seventh critically acclaimed novel...

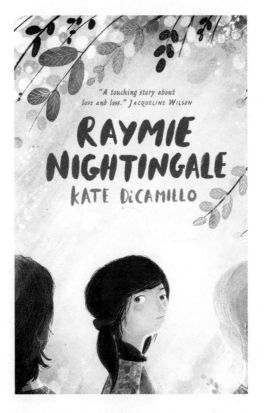

"As wise and tough and funny as it is beautiful. I loved it." Katherine Rundell, author of *Rooftoppers*